Little Lester the Christmas Donkey

by
Erin Wade
A Christmas Short Story
For Our
Amazing Grace

Little Lester the Christmas Donkey
by Erin Wade
ISBN: 9798303874183
Editor
Julie Versoi
Copyright 12/16/2024
By Erin Wade
All Rights Reserved
No part of this book may be reproduced,
without written permission from the author.
Published by
Wade Write Publishing
www.erinwade.us
Paperback

Little Lester the Christmas Donkey

Copyright ©12/2024 by Erin Wade
All rights reserved. No part of this book may be reproduced without written permission from the author.

COPYRIGHT NOTICE: All rights reserved under the International and Pan American Copyright Conventions. No part of this book may be reproduced or transmitted in any form or by any means, electronic or mechanical, including photocopying and recording, or by any information storage and retrieval system, without permission in writing from the author or publisher.

WARNING: The unauthorized reproduction or distribution of this copyrighted work is illegal. Criminal copyright infringement, including infringement without monetary gain, is investigated by the FBI and is punishable by up to five years in prison and a fine of $250,000.

THIS IS A WORK OF FICTION. Names, places, characters, and incidents are the product of the author's imagination or used fictitiously. Any resemblance to actual persons, living or dead, organizations, events, or locales is entirely coincidental.

DEDICATION

To my wife. You are the one with all the faith and a strong belief in miracles. Thanks to you I look forward to each day with awe and joy. You make me a better person. Life is sweeter with you.

Erin

ACKNOWLEDGEMENTS

A special "Thank You" to my wonderful witty friend and editor **Julie Versoi**. I treasure her advice and welcome her suggestions. She makes me a better storyteller.

Contents

Chapter 1 6
   Going Home 6
Chapter 2 11
   He Needs a Name 11
Chapter 3 15
   A Meeting of the Minds 15
Chapter 4 17
   A Friend in Need 17
Chapter 5 20
   A Believer 20
Chapter 6 23
   I Know His Name 23
Chapter 7 27
   I Don't Believe in Miracles 27
Chapter 8 32
   Memories 32

Do You Hear What I Hear?
Chapter 1 35
Chapter 2 38
Chapter 3 42
Chapter 4 46
Chapter 5 49
Chapter 6 53
Chapter 7 59
Chapter 8 62
Chapter 9 67

Little Lester the Christmas Donkey

Chapter 10 70
Chapter 11 73
Chapter 12 78
Chapter 13 81
Chapter 14 86
Chapter 15 90
Chapter 16 95

CHAPTER 1

Going Home

Veterinarian Emery Clark watched her wife and wondered how she could be so strong. Amy smiled and laughed as she talked with their daughter Leah, telling her about the baby ducks and tiny goats that were thriving on their farm.

Leah giggled and clapped her hands as she delighted in her mother's tales of animal adventures.

Emery turned away and stepped into the hall closing the door behind her. She wiped the tears from her eyes with the sleeve of her pullover. A gentle hand rested on her shoulder.

Dr. Laura Adams slipped her arm around the woman's shoulder and spoke softly. "This is Leah's last chemo treatment, Emery. We have done all we can do for her. It's in God's hands now."

Everything in Emery rebelled against the statement. *What kind of God put an eight-year-old through the suffering Leah had experienced? What kind of monster would torture a child that way?*

She straightened her shoulders and faced Dr. Adams. "How long does she have?"

"A week, two at the most," the doctor answered. "She keeps asking to go home for Christmas. You can take her home if you want. I think she will be happier at home with you and Amy."

Emery smiled. "We would like that. We want to savor every minute with her."

"I'll start the paperwork for her release, and you can take her home today. I want to prepare you; she may not make it until Christmas."

Emery brushed away her tears. "I need instructions," Emery pleaded. "I need to know what to watch for if she gets worse. What to do to keep her comfortable and pain free."

"To begin with, keep her warm. Be sure you keep her head covered in a soft cap. That will help hold her body heat."

"Yes," Emery agreed blinking back tears. "A little bald head doesn't hold much heat."

"I will send home her medications and detailed information on their use. If you need me anytime night or day, don't hesitate to call me."

Emery nodded, pulled herself together, put a big smile on her face, and returned to the hospital room. "Guess who is going home with Mommie and me today?"

A huge smile lit Leah's gaunt little face. "Me!" she squealed softly.

Amy smiled at her wife and gave her the look that always melted Emery's heart.

"When can we leave?" Leah asked.

"As soon as Dr. Adams gets us dismissed." Emery replied. "It is cold outside, so we need to bundle you up."

Amy hugged her daughter and hid the tears in her eyes.

Emery pulled Leah's clothes from the closet and placed them on the bed. "We will need to buy you some new clothes when you feel like shopping," she said. "These are too big for you right now, but with Mommie's home cooking I'm sure you will grow back into them."

Emery gathered all Leah's belongings and loaded them into her wife's car. She started it and pulled it to the front of the hospital door. She turned the heater on full blast then grabbed the wheelchair from the car's trunk and hurried to Leah's room.

It was dark when Emery lifted Leah into the passenger's seat beside Amy. "You two go ahead, I'll take care of checking out of the hospital, then follow you in the Jeep," Emery said as she lifted the wheelchair into the back of Amy's car.

##

Emery was almost home when Amy called her cellphone. "Honey, there is an injured animal on the side of the drive that turns into our ranch road. Leah is insisting on waiting for you. She won't leave it."

"Can you tell what it is?"

"It looks like a car has hit a colt or a deer. It is small and struggling to stand. It is starting to snow, and it will freeze to death if we don't help it."

"I'm right behind you. I see your taillights."

Emery pulled to a stop behind her wife's car and ran to Amy's window. The window lowered and Leah cried, "Mom, it's hurt. You've got to help it. Please."

"I will, sweetie. You and Mommie go to the house. I don't want you to get chilled."

As Amy's taillights disappeared, Emery grabbed a hypodermic needle from her bag and walked toward the struggling animal talking to it in soft reassuring tones.

"Easy little fellow. I'm here to help you."

As Emery approached, the animal ceased struggling and followed Emery's every move with large round eyes.

"You will be okay," Emery hummed soothingly as she approached the injured animal. "You're not a colt, you're a donkey! Where did you come from? No one around here has donkeys."

The donkey raised his head following Emery's movements with his big eyes.

"Can you stand?" Emery talked as she felt the animal's legs for breaks. "Nothing broken. Let's see if we can get you on your feet."

Moving slowly, Emery slipped her hands beneath the small donkey and lifted with all her strength. The animal flailed and struggled to get his feet under his body. To Emery's surprise, he made a final lunge and sprung to his feet. He staggered and leaned against the vet.

Emery gave a sigh of relief and placed her hand on his side. Letting him lean against her leg and holding her hand on his other side, she slowly walked him to the back of her Jeep. "This is where you must really trust me," she said as she reached under his stomach and lifted him into the air. To her surprise, he didn't flail or move a muscle trusting her to place him into the back of the vehicle. She was thankful she hadn't needed to sedate him.

"So far so good," she muttered as the small donkey quietly settled on the floor and leaned against the back of the seats.

Emery pulled her Jeep inside the barn and closed the door, then checked on the donkey. He was awake, but peaceful. She opened the door and gently lifted him to the ground. Still limping, he let her walk him to a bed of clean hay where he laid down heaving a sigh of exhaustion.

He let her clean and treat his cuts and rub liniment on his bruises. She gave him food and water then covered him with a horse blanket. "This should keep you warm," she said more to reassure herself than the animal.

Emery closed the door to the barn and ran to the house. It was snowing heavily and the lights from the kitchen window were a welcome sight.

CHAPTER 2

He Needs a Name

"Mom! Mom! Is he okay?" Leah called as Emery entered the kitchen door.

"He is going to be fine." Emery laughed at her daughter's enthusiasm. "You're sitting in a regular chair. Why aren't you in your wheelchair?"

"I feel so much better here at home." Leah exclaimed. "I feel stronger."

"That is wonderful." Emery smiled.

"I want to see him before I go to sleep," Leah begged.

"Not tonight, baby. It is snowing hard, and we can't chance you catching a cold." Emery hung her jacket on the coat hook and hugged Amy.

"Is it a colt or a deer?" Leah bombarded her mom with questions.

"Neither." Emery grinned. "He is a donkey."

"A donkey!" Leah exclaimed. "He needs a name. What should we name him?"

"Is he really okay?" Amy whispered.

"Yes, no broken bones, just a little sore and a few cuts. It looks like a car grazed him knocking him into the bar ditch."

"Then my prayers have been answered," Amy beamed.

For a donkey, but not for our baby, Emery thought bitterly. *What kind of clown is in charge of answering prayers?*

"I need to name him tonight," Leah declared. "Can you take photos of him with your phone and let me see what he looks like up close?"

"Of course," Emery agreed.

"You have time before dinner is ready," Amy assured her as Emery pulled on her jacket.

Emery dutifully took several photos of the donkey then tried to entice him with grain and water that he ignored. "You must eat to grow big and strong," Emery talked to the animal as she brushed his coat. "Who do you belong to little fellow?"

Emery's phone rang, making the donkey jump, but he settled down quickly when Amy's voice came over the speaker.

"Dinner is on the table," Amy announced.

"On my way, Babe," Emery said giving the donkey a final pat and pulling a blanket over him.

##

Little Lester the Christmas Donkey

During dinner Leah thumbed through the photos of the donkey on Emery's cellphone. "He looks so small," she exclaimed.

"He is a little fellow," Emery replied, "but strong for one so small. He's spunky - a lot like you."

Leah's eyes beamed as she listened to her mom describe the animal. "I can't wait to pet him," she exclaimed.

"When it gets warmer, hon," Emery patted her hand. "We can't chance you catching a cold."

"What should we name him?" Leah reiterated. "Henry or Bucky? No, they don't quite fit him. Maybe Leroy. No, I must pet him to know his name."

"It's past your bedtime." Amy smiled at her daughter. "We have some new books to read to you after you have a bath."

Emery nodded as she scooped Leah into her arms and carried her to the bedroom. She felt so frail and tiny in her arms. Emery blinked away the tears that threatened to fill her eyes.

Amy had a tub of warm water running by the time Emery reached the ensuite. Emery held their daughter as Amy undressed her. The site of her small skeletal body hit both of them hard as they tried to maintain a happy countenance. Amy pulled the warm cap from Leah's head and ran her hand through her short, cropped hair.

"Whoa, look at you, you're growing hair." Amy exclaimed.

Emery laughed. "You look like a baby chick."

Leah laughingly ran her hand over her head. "I do have hair!"

They played in the tub as they bathed their daughter. Emery kept her from slipping under the water as Amy washed her. Emery lifted her from the water and Amy wrapped a warm towel around her.

"Storybook time," Leah exclaimed.

"We have new books to read," Amy reminded Leah as Emery put the girl's pajamas on her.

"There, all nice and warm," Amy said as she pulled Leah into her arms. "You take a quick shower honey, and I'll start reading to our daughter."

Leah was sound asleep snuggled into her mother's side. "I think the excitement of the donkey has exhausted her," Amy confessed as Emery gently picked up the child and placed her in the bed next to theirs.

"I can't believe her hair is growing so fast," Emery ran her fingers through the girl's hair. "Must have something to do with the new meds."

Emery slipped into their bed and held her wife in her arms as Amy cried herself to sleep.

CHAPTER 3

A Meeting of the Minds

Emery lay awake thinking about the way Amy and Leah had become the most important people in her life. Amy had rushed into the animal hospital with a puppy that was half dead.

"Please, can you save her," Amy had begged Emery.

"What happened? Did a car run over her?" Emery had asked as she took the blood-soaked puppy to her exam room.

"My husband was angry with me and stomped her," Amy wailed. "He has always had a bad temper, but he has never been this cruel."

Emery felt the small dog's heart stop beating before she placed her on the exam table. "She is gone," she informed Amy, "There is nothing I can do."

Amy collapsed to her knees emitting a wail that slid into keening as her body swayed back and forth.

Emery frantically looked around for her assistant who was nowhere to be seen. The vet was used to dealing with distraught pet owners but had never seen anyone react so genuinely sorrowful. She tried to pull the heartbroken woman to her feet, but Amy's body went limp, and she slid to the floor.

Emery yelled for someone to help her, and the lab tech rushed to her assistance. The two of them managed to move Amy into Emery's office chair and prop her upright. Amy sucked air and choked. Emery got her a glass of water and let her sip it slowly.

"Are you okay?" Emery asked as Amy stopped gasping for air. "Are you hurt too."

"I am fine," Amy mumbled obviously embarrassed by her outbreak. "I just . . . can't believe he killed my dog. I hate him. I can't return home."

"Do you have relatives or friends I can call for you?" Emery inquired.

"No, we just moved here from California, and I don't know anyone." Amy began weeping again.

"I'm finished here for the day," Emery said. "Let me take you to dinner so you can calm down and think."

Amy's watery blue eyes stared at Emery. "I don't want to impose on you. You don't know me. Why would you help me?"

"Because you are another human in need of a friend," Emery answered honestly. "I guess you could say we bonded over our love for animals."

Chapter 4

A Friend in Need

Emery took Amy to a quiet restaurant where a large fireplace warmed the room. She learned that Amy and her husband had moved to their town to manage the local branch of his company.

"He is very smart and driven," Amy explained, "but he has a vicious temper I never saw while we dated. He was always so sweet and amiable. He changed completely after we moved here. I don't even know him."

"In California, did you have family and friends to provide you support?" Emery asked.

"Yes, but here I have no one, just him."

"So, he thinks he can treat you any way he wants," Emery surmised. "You have no one to turn to."

"Except a stranger." Tears welled up in Amy's eyes. "I don't know what to do."

"Do you have a job?"

"No, he doesn't want me to work."

"To make you dependent on him," Emery noted.

"That is what we argued over," Amy admitted. "I have an accounting degree and love working in that field. There is something about numbers that is so perfect and exact. I told him I wanted to get a job, and he went ballistic. He kicked my puppy and screamed that I didn't need it if I wasn't going to stay home and take care of it. Then he stomped it.

"When he left the room, I grabbed the puppy and came straight here."

"I am so sorry I couldn't…"

"I knew it was mortally injured," Amy admitted. "I just hoped I was wrong."

"What will you do?" Emery asked.

"I don't know. Is there a women's shelter in this town? Maybe I can stay there until I get a job and can afford my own place."

"I have an extra bedroom," Emery volunteered. "You are welcome to stay in my home tonight, if you'd like."

"You are very kind," Amy smiled. "Thank you. Hopefully, things will look brighter tomorrow."

"Our bookkeeper is leaving at the end of the month," Emery added. "Would you like the job?"

"I'd love it," Amy exclaimed. "You are surely an angel in disguise. You are too good to be true."

Emery laughed. "I'm no angel, but I do need a new bookkeeper."

##

A loud banging on her front door dragged Emery from a deep sleep. She pulled on her robe and staggered to the door. She checked the security camera to see who was beating down her door at 5:00 a.m. It was a tall muscular man.

She spoke into the intercom as she dialed 911. "What do you want?"

"My wife!" The man yelled.

"Who is your wife?"

"Amy Stafford. I know she is here. I tracked her cellphone. I am Jim Stafford, and I want to talk to her."

"Mr. Stafford, you can talk with her tomorrow," Emery replied. "I'm not opening this door, so you need to go home."

Stafford began kicking the door as the 911 dispatcher answered Emery's call. Emery gave her the address and told her a man was trying to kick down her door. Stafford was still banging on the door when a squad car pulled to the curb in front of Emery's house.

Two officers confronted Stafford and took him to the patrol car. One officer stayed at the car while the other returned to the door of Emery's home. She opened the door and told the officer about the incident with the puppy and that she had allowed Mrs. Stafford to spend the night in her spare bedroom.

"I can arrest him, if you want to file charges against him," the officer informed her.

"I don't want to make things any worse for Mrs. Stafford," Emery explained. "Can you just make him stay away from my home."

"I can put the fear of God into him," the officer smiled. "We will handle it. You have a good night's sleep—or what's left of it." He gave her his card and said goodnight.

CHAPTER 5

A Believer

It had been easy to fall in love with beautiful blonde-haired Amy Stafford. Emery was impressed by her knowledge of business practices and the quick way she picked up all the ins and outs of the financial operations of a veterinary clinic.

No one's doormat, Amy had filed for a divorce and gotten a restraining order against her husband. When his company learned of his behavior, they transferred him back to California.

They had been friends for three months when Amy confessed her feelings for Emery and was thankful to learn the vet loved her too.

Amy was a religious person with a strong belief in God. Emery went to church with her but had little faith in a higher power.

The fourth month of their relationship, Amy confessed that she might be pregnant. "I don't want Jim to know," Amy informed her. "I would be horrified to have him in a child's life."

"I doubt you will ever hear from him again," Emery surmised. "So, you must be four months along."

Amy nodded. "I am so sorry. I know you didn't sign up for a woman and a baby in your life."

"I'm thrilled," Emery assured her. "I love you, children, and animals. In that order."

"God has been so good to me," Amy declared. "He sent you to me."

"God had nothing to do with it," Emery declared. "I fell in love with you the minute I saw you. Even if you were howling like a dying banshee in my clinic."

When Leah was born, the nurse placed her in Emery's arms. "I was the first to hold Leah," she proudly told people.

Emery didn't hide the fact that Amy and Leah were her world. They purchased a small farm outside of town and everything was right in their perfect life. Emery was beginning to believe there was a God. She believed it for eight years until Leah was diagnosed with a fast-growing cancer.

When the doctors explained that they might be able to extend Leah's life, but could not cure her, Emery railed against a God that would take the thing she loved most in the world.

Amy steadfastly clung to her beliefs, prayer, and church. They attended every Sunday until Leah was no longer strong enough and was admitted to the ward of the children's hospital so she could be monitored around the clock. They took turns sitting with her. Emery took the night shift, and Amy was by their daughter's side during the day. And now they had brought her home so she could leave the world surrounded by the two women who loved her more than anything in the world.

God, Emery thought bitterly. *No God would let anyone as sweet and precious as Leah die.*

CHAPTER 6

I Know His Name

"Mom, Mom, wake up," Leah slipped under the covers as Emery pried open her eyelids and hugged her daughter.

"What are you doing up so early?"

"I know his name," the child said excitedly.

"Whose name?" Emery was still trying to catch up with her daughter's conversation.

"Our donkey. I know his name. It is the perfect name for him."

"Okay!" Emery laughed as Amy draped her arm over her and placed a hand on Leah. "Are you going to share it with us?"

"Little Lester," Leah declared. "His name is Little Lester."

Amy laughed and Emery had to join her. "Little Lester. Where did you come up with that name?" Amy asked.

"It just came to me in the night," Leah exclaimed. "I think God sent it to me."

Emery stiffened as Amy replied. "I'm certain he did, sweetie but it isn't even daylight yet. You need to go back to sleep."

"May I sleep with you?"

"Of course, you can." Amy breathed deeply as Leah crawled over Emery to snuggle between them.

"Is Little Lester warm enough?" Leah asked.

"I'm sure he is," Emery replied. "I put an extra horse blanket over him."

"I will pray for him," Leah mumbled as she slipped into sleep.

##

The smell of freshly brewed coffee and frying bacon welcomed Emery to a new day. She was surprised to find she was the only one still in bed. She dressed and joined her wife and daughter in the kitchen. Flames flickered in the fireplace warming the house and giving it a welcoming, cozy feeling. For a few moments Emery forgot their situation as she watched the loves of her life laughing and talking.

"Something smells awesome," Emery declared as she joined them.

"Mommie is making pancakes," Leah proclaimed. "My favorite breakfast food."

Little Lester the Christmas Donkey

Emery poured a cup of coffee and sat down on a stool at the kitchen island where Leah was perched on the countertop. "Mommie is the best cook in the world," she complimented her wife. "You and I are lucky to have her."

Leah giggled. "I know. I am lucky to have both of you. You are the best mommies ever."

"That is why God gave us the best little girl in the world," Amy replied.

Emery sipped her coffee enjoying the camaraderie of their family. "I have a riddle for you two," she said.

"I love your riddles," Leah clapped her hands.

"Why did the teddy bear say, 'No' to dessert?"

Leah furrowed her brow as she tried to think of an answer. "I don't know" She gave up.

"Because he was already stuffed!" The three of them howled in laughter as they shared Emery's silly jokes.

"I have one," Amy volunteered. "Why are spiders so smart?"

"Because they scare the jeebies out of people," Leah squealed as her parents joined in her laughter.

"Because they know how to find everything on the web!" Amy replied.

"That is a great one Mom. I'll have to remember it to tell the kids when I return to school."

Emery swallowed and tried to continue their gaiety, but it was difficult. "I should go check on Little Lester," she declared. "It snowed all night."

"Make sure he is warm," Leah reminded her. "We should bring him into the house so he can lay in front of the fireplace."

"I don't think that is a good idea," Emery replied, "but I will make certain he is warm."

##

Emery pulled the collar of her coat around her ears and trudged through the deep snow. It was bitterly cold, and a north wind was picking up. Maybe they should take Little Lester into the house.

The little donkey was still lying in the same position he had been in the night before. He hadn't eaten or drunk water. Emery tried to entice him, but the animal ignored her efforts. She checked his cuts and bruises and tried to get him to his feet, but he made no effort to help her. She wondered if he had internal injuries. She would have to get him to the clinic to x-ray him and find out, but all the roads were closed due to the snow. Finally, she put another horse blanket over him and tucked it around him to keep any drafts out.

Without thinking, she uttered a prayer, "God, please let him be okay."

Unchecked tears streamed down her cheeks. She cried until she couldn't cry any more. She cried for Leah and Little Lester but most of all she cried for Amy. Amy who wouldn't accept the inevitable. God, she loved Amy. She would do anything to take away the pain and suffering Amy would have to go through. She recalled how sorrowfully Amy had reacted to the puppy's death so long ago and dreaded the agony her wife would endure over the loss of their only child.

She dried her tears and slogged back to the house.

CHAPTER 7

I Don't Believe in Miracles

"Is Little Lester okay?" Leah asked as soon as Emery entered the house.

"Yes, he is doing great," Emery exaggerated.

"Is he eating and drinking?"

"Not as much as I'd like," Emery hedged not wanting to lie to her daughter.

Little Lester the Christmas Donkey

She ran her hand through Leah's hair. "Are you putting fertilizer on your head?" she teased. "Your hair is growing like crazy."

Leah giggled. "Of course not, silly. I think being home is making everything better."

"I know it is for us," Amy chimed in. "It is so good to have you back home."

They spent the day playing board games and talking about Little Lester. Leah was excited about the little donkey and kept begging Emery to take her to the barn.

"It is bitterly cold outside," Emery replied. "You can visit him when it gets warmer."

After dinner, Amy made a big bowl of popcorn, and they settled in front of the television to watch cartoons and eventually the weather.

"Blizzard conditions are expected to last through the night," the weatherman reported. "With winds reaching thirty-five mile per hour, visibility is almost zero."

"I can attest to that," Emery agreed. "I can't remember such severe cold."

Leah giggled. "Knock knock."

"Who's there?" Amy laughed.

"Scold." Leah replied.

"Scold who?"

"Scold outside, let me in." Leah doubled over with laughter. "I love knock knock jokes," she added.

The three of them huddled under a blanket and watched another cartoon before going to bed. "I'm worried about Little Lester," Leah declared as the wind howled around their house. "Are you sure he is warm enough?"

"I promise, he is fine," Emery replied.

"May I open one of my Christmas presents?" Leah asked.

"I don't know," Amy teased. "You're supposed to wait until Christmas morning."

"Please, Mommie?" Leah pleaded.

"Okay," Amy agreed.

"You are such a push over." Emery laughed.

"It will give her longer to enjoy it," Amy explained.

Emery nodded and turned away. Her daughter seemed to be better, but she knew it was only her imagination working overtime because she wanted it so badly.

"May I open the biggest one?" Leah asked.

"Sure," Emery replied handing the box to Amy who carried it to Leah.

The girls ripped the paper from the package then tried to rip the tape from the box. "A little help here, Mom." She wrinkled her nose at Emery who grabbed a knife from the kitchen to cut the tape.

"Oh my gosh," Leah squealed. "A giant teddy bear. I love it. Moms thank you so much. I've always wanted a life-sized teddy bear." She hugged her mothers thanking them profusely. "I'm going to sleep with it from now on."

##

They put on their warmest pajamas to ward off the cold. "I'm going to sleep in my bed with Teddy," Leah informed them. "He will keep me warm."

After the lights were turned off Leah began to pray thanking God for her wonderful parents. "And God, please let Little Lester be okay."

A pang tore at Emery's heart. She was worried about the small donkey too. It was never a good sign when she couldn't get an equine on its feet.

"Mom," Leah's small voice rang out in the darkness.

"What, dear?"

"Would you sacrifice yourself for someone you loved?"

"In a heartbeat," Emery answered. *If only I could. That is a deal I'd make with God.*

"I knew you would." Leah replied.

##

Little Lester the Christmas Donkey

The house was unusually cold when Emery awoke. Amy was nestled against her slumbering softly. She wondered if the power lines had gone down. She turned her head to check on Leah. It took her a minute to realize that the only form on the girl's bed was the teddy bear. She bolted upright searching the room.

"What's wrong?" Amy sat up clutching the blanket to her.

"Where's Leah?" Emery gasped.

Both women hit the floor running into the kitchen. The open concept floorplan allowed them an unobstructed view of the kitchen, dining room and living room. Leah was not in the area and the back door was open.

"Dear God, she has gone to see about that donkey," Emery blurted.

They threw on their clothes and trekked through the snow that was melting. The wind had stopped blowing and smaller footprints were headed toward the barn. When they entered the barn they were surprised and relieved to find their daughter asleep on top of Little Lester.

The donkey was alert and watched them as they approached. He didn't move as the girl on his back slumbered softly.

"Leah, honey," Amy touched her daughter's back, and the girl opened her eyes. Her cheeks were rosy, and her hair was long. She looked healthy.

"Mom, I had to save Little Lester. He was freezing. I know I don't have long to live, and I wanted to save him even if it meant I would die."

Tears rolled down her mother's faces as they gazed at the transformation that had taken place in their daughter. She was the epitome of good health.

Leah slid from Little Lester's back and stood to face her parents. "I think I saved his life," she declared as the donkey stood up for the first time since they had found him on the side of the road. He ate the grain he had been ignoring and drank water.

"This is a miracle," Amy declared as she hugged her daughter.

"I know," Leah agreed. "He was almost dead when I came in here. I laid on him to keep him warm."

"I mean you! You look wonderful."

Emery pulled the collar of Leah's wrap back to examine the awful port in her chest. It was gone. The girl was no longer frail and ghostly white. It was as if she'd never had the horrible debilitating disease that had threatened to take her from them.

"She's healed," Emery choked. "She's well."

Amy pulled Leah into her arms and cried openly. "Thank you, God. Thank you."

"I have never believed in miracles," Emery said, "but I was wrong."

Little Lester rubbed his muzzle against Leah's arm, and she stroked his head. "Can we take him into the house?" she asked.

"Of course, you can," her mothers chimed.

CHAPTER 8

Memories

Little Lester watched the family through the window. He was happy. Leah was healed and her mothers were ecstatic.

He had been involved in many miracles over the centuries. He was thrilled to carry Mary the seventy miles from Nazareth to Bethlehem. He had walked his smoothest gait because Mary was with child and could deliver any minute. He had stood by patiently as Joseph had secured them a place to sleep in the stables of Bethlehem because there was no room for the family in the inn.

His heart almost burst with pride when the baby was born and visitors from faraway lands followed a star to bring him gifts. Shepherds had followed the same star to worship the child.

As the baby boy aged, he was known by many names and the miracles he performed. Lester knew what was expected of him when the man came for him. He was to carry the Nazarene triumphantly into Jerusalem where the man would be hailed as the prophesied savior, the descendant from the house of David. A huge crowd met him outside the city gates, spreading their cloaks on the road and cutting tree branches to spread on the path ahead of him. When people asked who the man was, the crowd answered, "This is Jesus, the prophet from Nazareth in Galilee."

Lester had proudly carried the man through the gates of the city not knowing he was carrying Jesus to his death. He couldn't get over his part in the crucifixion of Jesus. He was thankful that he was included in Jesus' life, but distraught that he had delivered him into the hands of his executioners. He wasn't allowed to run away with Jesus—to save him. He had to leave him in the hands of those who wished to crucify him.

To reward Lester for his faithfulness, God now allowed him to select one person per year to save. He had chosen Leah because of Amy's faith.

Often called "the beast of burden," Little Lester didn't feel burdened, he felt joyful. He took one last look at Leah then ascended into heaven as "Joy to the World" echoed all over earth.

The End

Do You Hear What I Hear?
A Christmas Short Story
By Erin Wade
Edited by Martha Hammer

ISBN: 9781674622842
©12/2019 Erin Wade
www.erinwade.us
Independently published
By Erin Wade

Do You Hear What I Hear? is a work of fiction. Names, characters, businesses, places, events and incidents are the products of the author's imagination or used in a fictitious manner. Any resemblance to actual persons, living or dead, or actual events is purely coincidental.

Copyright 2019 Erin Wade
All Rights Reserved

No part of this publication may be reproduced, stored in a retrieval system, or transmitted in any form or by any means—mechanical, photocopy, electronic, recording, or any other, except for brief quotations in printed reviews—without prior permission of the author.

Chapter 1

Kaden Snow pitched the police report onto the front seat of her car and headed toward the Oakmont Ninth-grade campus. She hated cases like the one she'd just been handed especially this close to Christmas.

Patrol cars and uniformed police officers were blocking the doors to the school's gym. The crime scene investigators pulled up as officers began stringing crime scene tape across the front of the gym entrance.

Thank God they aren't in the coroner's van, Kaden thought opening her car door and automatically checking for her holstered gun. She opened the back door of her vehicle and Boss jumped to the ground.

Boss was a two-year old Rottweiler. His bite was worse than his bark and he could take down and subdue a two-hundred-pound man faster than Kaden could pull her gun. Boss had saved her life on more than one occasion.

Boss stood motionless until Kaden snapped the leash onto his collar then he trotted beside her as she approached the officer in charge.

Officer Danny Raye greeted Kaden and gave her the rundown on the situation.

Elise Mason, a fifteen-year-old female student was missing. Her ripped clothing including her panties and bra had been found under the gym bleachers. Her cellphone had been crushed. Her mother had arrived at the school looking for her when she didn't ride the bus home.

Kaden walked to the CSI agent and watched as she photographed the girl's clothing. The school uniform consisted of a red polo shirt and a plaid skirt.

"Neatly folded with the panties and bra on top," Kaden noted. "Victim's clothes are usually scattered all over the crime scene."

Little Lester the Christmas Donkey

"Yeah," Lynn Brady snorted. "Whoever took the girl was a neat freak. No blood trails. No evidence of a struggle. Just a naked girl vanished into thin air."

"I'm going to give Boss the lead and see if he finds a trail," Kaden picked up the girl's panties and let Boss sniff them.

Boss put his head down and ran toward the school dumpsters. "Dear God," Kaden prayed, "don't let her be in one of those."

Boss sniffed the first two dumpsters then made a dive for the last one. He stood on his hind legs and stretched as far as he could pawing at the sliding door.

Kaden slid the metal door back and Boss dove into the dumpster before she could stop him. Officers and school officials gathered around the dumpster as Boss dug into the trash inside it.

After a few minutes Boss stuck his head out the side opening of the container. He was holding a Nike athletic shoe.

"Oh no," Officer Raye gasped. "Do you think she's in the dumpster?"

"There's only one way for you to find out," Kaden flashed an evil grin.

"You want me to climb in there?" Raye asked.

"Better you than me," Kaden shrugged. "I've got to talk to the parents and school officials. I'd rather not smell like a garbage dump."

Raye groaned then hosted himself into the dumpster. After rummaging around and encouraging Boss to find the girl he reported. "I found her other shoe, but she's not in here."

Kaden exhaled loudly. "That's good to know."

She stepped back as Boss and Raye jumped from the dumpster. "Oh, Boss, I'm going to have to bathe you tonight."

"How about me?" Raye grinned impishly. "I jumped into the dumpster for you too."

"I think you're old enough to bathe yourself," Kaden laughed.

Kaden carried the shoes to Lynn Brady. "I'll have my folks take the dumpster to the lab," Lynn volunteered. "Maybe we'll find something to identify the perp."

"Let me know if you do," Kaden said. "I'm going to start interviewing school employees."

Chapter 2

Kaden looked around for a school official and spotted Ashley Benton, Oakmont's prim and proper principal. Kaden had interacted with Ashley on several occasions. Benton was always polite but distant. She walked to Ashley. "Is there some place where we can talk?" Kaden asked.

"My office," Ashley replied leading the way into the school building.

"I'll put Boss back into the car," Kaden volunteered. "He doesn't smell so good after his dumpster diving."

"Nonsense," Ashley huffed. "Bring him with you."

"What time did the teachers discover Elise was missing?" Kaden asked leaning down to pat Boss on the head before following Ashley.

##

Ashley sat down at her computer and began typing. "It looks like she never showed up for fifth period which starts at one right after lunch. Her best friend came to the office at three-thirty when she failed to meet her at the bus. That's when we started looking for Elise."

"I need to speak with her best friend," Kaden said.

"I have everyone I thought you might want to speak with in the library," Ashley stood. "I'll get her."

"Bring her parents too," Kaden instructed. "She's a minor. I can't talk to her alone. If you don't mind, I'd appreciate it if you'd be present for the interviews."

Susie Freeman hesitantly entered the principal's office with her parents following close behind.

"Hi Susie," Kaden held out her hand trying to put the teenager at ease. "I'm Detective Kaden Snow. I need to ask you a few questions about Elise."

Susie nodded and sat down before her knees buckled. "I don't know anything," she blurted. "I just missed her this afternoon and feared something was wrong."

Ashley Benton observed the detective as she casually questioned Susie. Kaden Snow was about as hot as any woman Ashley had ever seen. Thick blonde hair danced on her shoulders as she turned her head from side to side sometimes tilting it in a questioning way. Blue eyes flashed when she couldn't connect the dots on Susie's answers.

"Did you have lunch with Elise?" Kaden asked.

"Um, I think so," Susie hedged.

"You're not sure?" Kaden raised a brow.

"I . . . was with her, but we didn't eat lunch," Susie explained.

"What did you do?" Kaden pushed.

"I . . . um. We . . . went to our gym lockers," Susie stuttered.

"Why?" Kaden barked.

"I . . . I don't remember," Susie began to cry.

"Did Elise meet a boyfriend?" Kaden guessed.

"Yeah," Susie grunted. "Her boyfriend."

"Did she leave campus with him?" Kaden coaxed.

"No," Susie declared. "Elise would never do that."

"Then why did you go to your lockers and where'd Elise go?" Kaden demanded. "I need to know Susie."

"I don't know," Susie began sobbing loudly. "I truly don't know."

"I think that's enough for now," Susie's mother stepped between her daughter and Kaden.

"I need to speak with Elise's parents," Kaden informed Ashley.

The principal escorted Susie Freeman and her parents from the room.

God, I hate a case like this, Kaden thought. *Especially during the Christmas holidays. Things fall through the cracks over the holidays.*

Thomas and Marlene Mason were obviously distraught but eager to help in any way they could.

"Susie said Elise had a boyfriend," Kaden informed them. "Do you know his name?"

"She may have a friend who is a boy here at school," Marlene replied, "but she didn't date anyone or have a real boyfriend."

"She's not allowed to date yet," Calvin added.

"Is her chrome book here on campus?" Kaden asked Ashley.

"I'll see if I can locate it," Ashly muttered typing into her computer. "It appears to be in her hall locker."

"I need it," Kaden quipped. "I'll need to have our forensic folks look at it."

Kaden turned to the Mason's, "If she has a computer at home, I'll need it too. I'll have an officer follow you home and pick it up."

"She has a laptop," Marlene nodded.

"Do you think she sneaked around and became involved with some pervert online?" Calvin choked.

"It's because you're so strict on her," Marlene accused her husband. "She's old enough to have boyfriends to the house."

"Already you're putting the blame on me," Calvin growled. "Typical. You're the one that lets her get on Facebook where all the perverts are."

"I'm not sure there's any blame needed," Kaden tried to calm the quarreling parents. "We're not certain what's going on. Please let the officer follow you home and get her laptop."

Mrs. Mason hugged Ashley goodbye and waited for Kaden to get a patrolman to follow them home. "Pick up the girl's computer and take it to Lynn Brady," Kaden instructed.

##

The sun had gone down, and the night had gotten colder. A bitter north wind ripped through Kaden's London Fog coat as if it were netting. She started her car turning the heater on high to warm it up then dashed back inside to get Boss.

CSI was still processing every fingerprint under the bleachers and Ashley Benton was giving instructions to the custodial employees.

Kaden waited for the principal. "I thought you might like a ride to your car," she chatted as they headed toward the door. "I'm right outside the door and my car is warm."

"Sold to the woman with a warm car," Ashley laughed. "Thank you."

Kaden drove to the other side of the school building and waited while Ashley cranked her car. To her dismay the auto chugged once, died, and refused to make another sound.

Kaden waved Ashley back into her car. Ashley ran back to the warmth of Kaden's vehicle cursing under her breath.

"I need to call a tow truck," Ashley worried her bottom lip with her teeth. "I just had my car worked on."

"Let me take you home," Kaden offered. "It sounds like a dead battery. I'll bring a new one in the morning and install it for you. A tow truck will cost you a small fortune not to mention the wait in this weather."

"Thank you, again," Ashley responded.

"My pleasure," Kaden snickered. "Would you like to join Boss and me for dinner? This weather is just begging us to eat barbeque."

"That does sound good," Ashley agreed. "I'd love a nice hot cup of coffee too."

"Barbeque it is," Kaden laughed.

Chapter 3

"Can you share your thoughts on Elise's disappearance?" Ashley asked as she warmed her hands on the hot coffee mug.

"Something's not adding up," Kaden stated. "I'll know more after we go through her computers. Too often girls her age meet some creep on the internet, think they're in love and agree to meet him only to find out they're meeting an old pedophile instead of a handsome young man."

"Thousands of girls and boys end up in the sex traffic trade because they were stupid enough to fall for someone they never met. The internet's a dangerous place for teenagers. Parents need to be more vigilant."

Ashley started to speak but was interrupted by her cellphone ringing. She answered it. "Yes, I'm having dinner and should be home in an hour . . . No, I'm not . . . I know my car's still at school. It wouldn't start. A police detective has given me a ride home and we stopped for dinner . . . Logan's Barbeque."

Kaden could tell by the look on Ashley's face that the person on the other end of the line was being unpleasant.

"I really must go," Ashley mumbled as the server placed their food in front of them.

"Something has come up," Kaden explained to the server. "May we have everything to go, please?"

"I'm sorry," Ashley said. "My husband's worried about me."

"I can understand that," Kaden said. "You're a beautiful woman and the weather's bad. No problem, I'll have you home in twenty minutes. We can finish our coffee while she boxes our dinner to go."

Ashley nodded and sipped her coffee.

They collected their to-go bags and ran to the car.

"What's your address?" Kaden asked waiting to give her GPS instructions. She typed in the street and number as Ashley rattled it off, then backed from the parking lot. They rode in silence until they reached Ashley's home.

"I'll give you a report tomorrow," Kaden said as she pulled into the driveway. "Hopefully we'll find something on the computers."

"Thank you," Ashley smiled, "for everything." She collected her things, and the food then ran into her house.

Kaden watched as Chelsea refilled her cup for the third time. "Your breakfast will be up in just a minute," the petite blonde informed her. "What brings you out so early on a day like this?"

"A friend's battery went dead last night," Kaden informed the waitress. "I ran by and picked up a new one this morning. I decided to have breakfast before facing the weather."

The local news station began its report on Elise's disappearance. What facts they didn't have they made up. Kaden shook her head in disbelief and ate her breakfast.

##

The tardy bell rang as Kaden entered the school offices. Students and teachers were scurrying in every direction. Kaden was always amazed at how quickly a school hallway could go from total bedlam to complete silence in less than thirty seconds.

"I need to see Principal Benton," Kaden informed the secretary as she signed the visitors form and flashed her badge.

"She's in her office," the secretary replied. "You can go in."

Kaden walked past the vice-principal giving the morning's announcements and opened the door to Ashley's office. The beautiful brunette was staring out her window. She jumped when Kaden closed the door.

"Oh," Ashley tittered, "you startled me." She didn't turn to face Kaden.

"I need your car keys," Kaden reminded her. "I have a new battery for you."

"They're on my desk," Ashley responded.

Kaden picked up the keys and walked around the desk to face Ashley. She was surprised to see the principal had a black eye.

"What happened?" Kaden asked.

"I slipped and fell this morning," Ashley smiled slightly, and Kaden saw the cut on her bottom lip.

"I'll just take care of the car for you," Kaden pitched the keys into the air and easily caught them. "I'll be back in a jiffy."

##

As Kaden switched out the batteries she wondered if Bryan Benton had hit his wife. Kaden had seen her share of wife abuse during her time on the force and could easily spot a fist to a woman's eye.

Kaden took Ashley's keys back to her office and asked to see Elise Mason's gym locker.

"I'll have someone take you to her locker," Ashley said.

"I want you to take me," Kaden insisted.

Ashley nodded and dragged the master keys from her desk. "Follow me," she commanded. "What are you looking for?"

"I have a hard time believing anyone would kidnap a girl naked especially in this weather," Kaden replied. "I want to see if her gym clothes are gone."

Ashley raised her perfectly arched brow then grimaced at the pain of the involuntary action.

Just as Kaden had surmised, Elise's gym clothes were gone. "Did she have an extra pair of shoes in her locker?" Kaden asked.

"Yes," Ashley said. "The students must wear a particular gym shoe to avoid scratching the new gym floor."

"I'm beginning to think this a run-away instead of a kidnapping," Kaden noted. She called Lynn Brady.

"Lynn can you send someone to process the Mason girl's gym locker?" Kaden asked.

"They'll be there in about an hour," Lynn answered.

"Is it okay if I cool my heels in your office until CSI gets here?" Kaden asked. "Or even better let's start your car and drive it to the Brunch House for a good cup of coffee."

"Let me go to the powder room first," Ashley nodded.

Kaden walked to the vice-principal's office and introduced herself. She made small talk then discreetly asked if Ashley was accident prone.

The vice principal studied Kaden for a few seconds then closed her office door. "Her husband beats her," she blurted.

"I thought so," Kaden muttered. "Thanks for not playing games with me." She opened the door and stepped into the hallway as Ashley walked from her office.

Chapter 4

Ashley had reapplied makeup and covered her black eye nicely. One had to look closely to see the dark shadow beneath the makeup.

"Do you want to discuss the elephant at our table?" Kaden asked stirring cream into her coffee.

"I'd rather talk about the Christmas Pageant our drama department is preparing for the district," Ashley smiled.

"Your call, Principal Benton," Kaden shrugged.

Kaden listened patiently as Ashley described the manger scene of the upcoming drama production.

"Are you allowed to do that?" Kaden asked.

"What do you mean?" Ashley scowled.

"Present Christ's birth to public school children," Kaden frowned. "I thought there was a prohibition against anything religious being tied to Christmas. For instance, schools no longer have "Christmas Concerts." They have "Winter Concerts."

"I've done this program every year," Ashley smiled. "So far I haven't been reprimanded or fired. We also say a morning prayer."

"You're bucking the entire school system," Kaden pointed out, "yet you won't stand up to a husband who—"

"Detective Snow," Ashley barked, "you have no idea what you're talking about."

"Ashley, I worked domestic violence for three years, I know—" Kaden tried again.

"Please take me back to the school," Ashley glowered.

##

The trip back to the school was as icy in the car as the snow was outside it. Kaden dropped Ashley off in front of the school then drove to the back door that accessed the gym. Despite the cold weather, CSI had the door propped open. Two agents were lifting fingerprints from Elise's locker.

"We found traces of blood," one of the agents informed Kaden. "We'll run DNA on it and see who it belongs to."

Kaden was about to ask why they had the door open when her phone rang, and she answered it.

"Detective Snow, this is dispatch. Holy Cross Methodist Hospital just called. They have your missing girl in the emergency room."

"Thanks," Kaden said, "I'm on my way. Has the hospital notified her parents?"

"I think so," dispatch replied. "I'm not sure."

##

Snow was beginning to cover the ground when Kaden reached the hospital. She valet parked her car and hurried to the warmth inside the ten-story structure. Holy Cross was warm and inviting. The vast lobby was beautifully decorated with Christmas Trees and lights. A manger scene covered one end of the waiting room. *Funny how hard people work to make a place of sadness look happy*, Kaden thought.

"May I have the room number for Elise Mason?" Kaden asked pulling back her coat to expose the badge clipped to her belt.

"I'm sorry, I don't have a Mason," the volunteer replied. "When was she admitted?"

"Sometime today," Kaden frowned.

"I have a female Jane Doe," the woman responded.

"That would be her," Kaden nodded.

The volunteer wrote the room number on a sticky note and handed it to Kaden.

When the elevator door opened the Mason's stepped out. Mrs. Mason was sobbing loudly.

Elise is dead, Kaden thought. "Elise?" Kaden said.

"The girl is dead," Mr. Mason shook his head. "But she's not Elise."

Relief flooded Kaden. She felt guilty. Some poor girl was dead, but her joy at knowing Elise might still be alive was overwhelming.

"I'm so happy to hear that," Kaden consoled the Mason's.

"Yeah, we made a trip for nothing," Calvin grumbled. "This weather is—"

"Are you angry because Elise isn't lying up there dead?" Marlene shrieked. "You're a real piece of work Calvin."

"Mr. and Mrs. Mason, please," Kaden begged. "I know how difficult this is, but you need to console each other at a time like this."

The Mason's looked properly embarrassed and walked away.

Since I'm here, Kaden thought. She overcame her reluctance to mettle in others' affairs and took the elevator to the administrative floor of the hospital. She intended to take advantage of the friendships she had cultivated during her years on the domestic violence unit.

"Casey," Kaden greeted her friend. "I need some information on a patient and before you ask, I have no warrant or subpoena. Just an imposition on our friendship."

Casey laughed. "What else is new, Kaden?"

"I'm not going to lie to you," Kaden admitted sliding a scrap of paper to her friend. "I'm checking on a friend."

Casey read the name on the note. "The ninth-grade principal," she whispered.

Kaden nodded and waited as Casey searched the hospital's database.

"Nope, nada," Casey shrugged. "She's never been in Holy Cross."

"Good," Kaden exclaimed. "Occasionally, I like it when I'm wrong."

Chapter 5

"Talk dirty to me, Lynn," Kaden grinned at the pretty ME. "Give me a lead, any lead will do."

"Every kid in that school has fingered Elise's locker," Lynn declared. "We tracked all the fingerprints back to students except for two. Two very nasty characters, the Leland brothers."

Kaden inhaled deeply reaching for the report Lynn held out to her. Cletus and Curtis Leland were known pedophiles. On parole for sexual assault of a minor, they were forbidden access to all school campuses, yet they had been on the grounds and in the buildings of the Oakmont campus

"We'll bring them in," Kaden declared as she left the CSI lab heading to her captain's office.

Captain Jeff Token waved Kaden into his office as he hung up his phone. "What's up, Kaden?"

Kaden read him in on the case. "I want to arrest them," she ended. "Even if they aren't involved in this case, they've broken the terms of their parole and need to be locked up."

"Their fingerprints inside a public school gives us grounds for arrest," Token agreed. "Get a warrant and take Bevo with you."

Bevo Warren was a former Dallas Cowboy tackle. Standing six-foot five and weighing two-hundred and fifty pounds, Bevo was strong as a bull and almost as fast. Taking Bevo was like using a tank to swat a fly, but Kaden welcomed the big guy's company.

##

"Pedophiles," Bevo snorted. "I hope they resist arrest."

"If they do," Kaden laughed, "they're all yours."

Little Lester the Christmas Donkey

When they arrived at the home of the Leland brothers, the lights were on, and Kaden could see the flickering TV through the window.

"I'll take the back door," Bevo whispered. "Just drive 'em my way baby girl."

True to form, when Kaden banged on the front door and yelled, "Police, open up," the Leland's ran out the back door and right into the fists of Bevo. Both were out cold when Kaden joined her partner. They handcuffed the men and Bevo heaped snow onto their heads bringing them to.

Both men tried to stand but couldn't get their balance with their hands cuffed behind them. They shook the snow from their heads, cursing violently as Bevo pulled them to their feet.

##

After three hours of intense interrogation, Cletus began to cry. "We ain't got that girl," he declared.

"Look Cletus," Kaden drawled, "I must turn you over to Bevo. Curtis is unconscious and Bevo wants a go at you."

"I know nothing," Cletus whined.

The interrogation door opened and Bevo dominated the room. "Give me five minutes with him," Bevo pleaded. "He'll either talk or die and honestly I don't care which one it is."

"I don't know anything," Cletus whimpered. "You've got the wrong guys."

Bam! It sounded like a gun shot when Bevo slammed his fist against the table. "You lying piece of shit," he bellowed. "We've got your fingerprints on the girl's locker. We have chatroom conversations where you and Curtis took turns wooing her over the internet. Your ugly van was recorded by the school security cameras driving by the school"

"Yes, yes, we did that," Cletus sobbed, "but we never kidnapped her."

"What were you doing in the school gym—in the girl's locker?" Bevo raged.

"We . . . we stole her panties," Cletus squeaked.

"You stole her panties," Bevo growled. "You spent months courting her through the internet just to steal her panties."

Bevo turned to Kaden. "Do I look stupid to you?" He demanded. "I mean do I look stupid enough to swallow the pile of crap Cletus is trying to feed me?"

"No-o-o," Kaden drawled again.

"I'm gonna' hurt him," Bevo whispered loudly.

"I'm gonna' get a cup of coffee," Kaden walked toward the door. "I'll be back in an hour or so. Try to complete your interrogation by then."

"Wait! Wait!" Cletus shrieked. "Don't leave me alone with him. He'll kill me."

"One can only hope," Kaden grinned evilly as she opened the door.

"I'll talk," Cletus choked. "I'll tell you everything."

Kaden returned to the interrogation table and pushed the button under the table that turned on the video recorder.

"Cletus Leland you wish to give us a statement of your own freewill?" Kaden asked.

Cletus' eyes darted around the room. "Yes, I wish to do that."

"Go ahead," Kaden invited.

"Curtis and I have been interacting with the Mason girl for about six months," Cletus began his confession.

"Stupidly she gave us her real name and where she attended school. It was easy to find her. She didn't realize she was communicating with two men. She thought we were just one teenage boy from the next town over.

"She was so easy. She was scared her parents were going to divorce and we consoled her telling her we had experienced that and knew how she felt.

"We finally convinced her to play hooky from school. She agreed to let us pick her up outside the gym. When she saw the van and realized I was older than she thought, she ran back into the gym. We chased her and caught her at her locker. Our prints should only be on the outside of the locker door. She ran out of the gym, and we ran back to our van. I swear that's the last we saw of her."

Kaden pushed a yellow notepad and a pen to Cletus. "Write it all down."

The two officers left the room.

"I need to call Lynn," Kaden said dialing the ME's number. "Lynn, where were the Leland brothers prints on Elise's locker?" She waited while Lynn double checked the location of the prints.

"Outside front of the locker door," Lynn answered.

"Damn," Kaden muttered. "Thanks."

"I think Cletus is telling the truth," Kaden scowled. "Lynn said the prints were only on the outside door."

"Then where's the girl?" Bevo huffed.

"I don't know," Kaden sighed. "Let's book the two creeps for parole violation. I'll follow up and make certain they return to the pen to serve their sentences."

Chapter 6

Kaden was having a difficult time driving the image of Ashley Benton's black eye from her mind. She decided to drop by the school on the pretense of reporting their progress—or lack of—to the pretty principal. She parked behind the school next to Ashley's car.

The secretary greeted Kaden as she entered the office. "Principal Benton's in her office," she announced. "She's expecting you."

Kaden knocked on Ashley's door and opened it when "Come in." Came from the principal.

"Hey," Ashley smiled, "I thought I'd drop in and give you an update on the case."

She spent the next half hour relating the events of her day regarding her search for Elise. She didn't mention checking on Ashley's hospital records.

"We're leaving," the secretary informed Ashley as she turned out the main lights in the office. "See you in the morning."

"Have you eaten dinner?" Ashley asked gathering her computer and purse.

"No," Kaden answered.

"Do you mind dining with me?" Ashley smiled.

"I don't mind," Kaden answered thoughtfully. "I'm under the impression I got you in trouble last night by going to dinner with you."

"Oh, no, that was just a misunderstanding," Ashley waved her hand dismissively.

"You're sure your husband won't mind?" Kaden clarified.

"Bryan's out of town," Ashley explained. "He'll be in Washington overnight."

"In that case, I'd be delighted to keep you company." Kaden laughed.

"My car's out back," Ashley said as Kaden held her coat so she could slide into it. "We can leave through the gym door. It'll automatically lock behind us."

"Let me carry that," Kaden slid Ashley's computer strap from the principal's shoulder to her own.

Ashley talked about her day as they walked down the silent hallways.

"This place is eerie without the students," Kaden noted. "Do you often work here alone at night?"

"Sometimes," Ashley admitted. "It is kind of creepy."

Kaden laughed and realized that Ashley was laughing for the first time. "Your eyes sparkle when you laugh," Kaden said.

"As do yours Miss Tough Detective," Ashley teased. "You're really very beautiful."

"Thank you," Kaden blushed.

"You're blushing," Ashley laughed again.

"It's a blonde thing," Kaden grinned.

Kaden held open the gym door allowing Ashley to precede her into the cavernous room. A dim light at each end of the gym cast shadows across the floor. Ashley slipped her hand through Kaden's arm and tucked in close to her side.

Kaden admitted she liked the feel of the pretty brunette snugged tight against her. She allowed herself to become lost in the closeness of Ashley Benton.

"Do you hear what I hear?" Ashley whispered.

They stopped in the center of the gym floor and listened for the sound but heard nothing. "Probably just the custodians vacuuming," Ashley dismissed the uneasy feeling that had settled over her.

Kaden unsnapped the strap that secured her Glock in its holster. By the time they reached the gym door she was feeling foolish about being spooked so easily. She prepared herself for the cold blast of air she knew would hit them when she opened the gym door.

"I'll follow you," Kaden leaned down and spoke into Ashley's ear. "Wherever you want to dine is fine with me."

Kaden put the computer bag into Ashley's back seat then sprinted to her own car. She didn't feel the cold. The heat of brushing her lips against Ashley's ear and inhaling the scent of her hair had caught Kaden by surprise. She knew Ashley felt it too from the way the brunette had stiffened and softly moaned.

Kaden fought to control the feeling settling in the pit of her stomach. Ashley Benton was a married woman. *There's not a lesbian bone in her body*, Kaden thought. *But she did react to me.* Another thought slipped through her mind.

##

Ashley parked her car as close as possible to the entrance of an Outback Steakhouse and sprinted inside. Kaden quickly followed her brushing the snow from her coat.

"Whoa," Kaden inhaled as the restaurant door closed behind her. "It's colder than a well digger's . . . uh, um—"

Ashley laughed at the detective's failure to complete a sentence that could have been offensive. "Posterior?" Ashley finished the idiom.

"Yes," Kaden chuckled following the hostess to a table in a secluded corner of the establishment.

"Oh, I like this," Ashley said suggestively. "Hiding in shadowy corners."

"We have no reason to hide," Kaden chided. *Yet*! She thought.

"I was playing with you," Ashley glanced away from the look in Kaden's eyes. "They have excellent prime rib here."

They sat across the table from each other and began sharing their life stories. "What made you choose a career in education?" Kaden asked.

"Probably the same reason you chose a career in law enforcement," Ashley responded. "I wanted to make a difference."

"And have you?" Kaden asked.

"I like to think so," Ashley shrugged. "But when one of my students is kidnapped from my campus, I have to wonder."

"You're young for a school principal," Kaden noted.

"I'm probably not as young as you think," Ashley laughed. "It's because I'm short. People tend to think a five-foot-two person is a youngster."

"I have noticed many of your students tower over you," Kaden chuckled. "But you have a presence about you that demands respect—a hard core. I like that."

Kaden smiled as she listened to Ashley's funny anecdotes. *She probably weighs a hundred and five pounds soaking wet,* she thought. She found herself wanting to protect the petite woman from life's slings and arrows. *From her husband,* the thought came out of nowhere and made Kaden jerk.

"Are you okay?" Ashley asked.

"What?" Kaden quipped pulling her thoughts back to the present.

"Your body jerked," Ashley frowned. "You must be exhausted. It was thoughtless of me to insist that you have dinner with me."

"Oh, no," Kaden assured her. "my mind just wandered to Elise. The longer it takes us to find her the less chance we have of finding her alive.

"I'm certain Susie Freeman knows something she isn't telling me. I plan to question her again tomorrow. I'll give her parents the choice of meeting me at school or bringing her to the station."

"I'm sure they'll choose to bring her to the school," Ashley said. "Do you want me to be present?"

"If it's not too much trouble," Kaden replied. "I'd like your input."

"I assume you began your career as a teacher," Kaden steered the conversation toward a happier topic.

"Yes, second grade," Ashley smiled. "That was a rude awakening. I love that age, but it's distressing how little attention parents pay their children and how undisciplined some of the little ones are.

"I was surprised to learn that every campus has a person that is certified to restrain children. Some of the students are so violent they must be restrained for the protection of other students."

"Wow and I think my job's difficult," Kaden scowled. "Obviously you didn't stay in elementary school."

"No, I worked on my masters and doctorate in administration while I taught grade school then taught middle school a few years. When the district built the ninth-grade campus I was offered my current job. I've been principal for five years and I love it."

"And somewhere in there you found the time to marry Bryan Benton," Kaden noted as the server placed their orders on the table.

"Yes," Ashley flinched.

Kaden cut two slices from the hot bread and pushed the cutting board toward Ashley.

"Thank you," Ashley smiled taking a slice and buttering it. "What about you? How long have you been in law enforcement?"

"I graduated with a degree in criminal law," Kaden answered. "Then I decided to suck it up and do three more years for my law degree. I worked in the district attorney's office for a couple of years but discovered I preferred catching criminals instead of sitting behind a desk and negotiating plea bargains with them. From my time in the DA's office, I learned how to put together a solid case that required little work on the prosecutor's part. If I give them a slam-dunk case the perp usually goes to prison. I much prefer that to plea bargaining.

"I spent a couple of years in patrol then domestic violence and now I'm the lead detective in CID. I love my work except for cases like this one."

They talked until closing time laughing at each other's stories and sharing glimpses of their dreams.

"How about a photo, ladies," a professional photographer hired for the holidays approached the two.

"I don't think so." Ashley smiled.

"I'll shoot each of you. Photos make great Christmas gifts. Your mother's will love it."

"Why not?" Kaden laughed. "It'll be fun."

The man took several shots of each of them then handed them his card. "Just go on that website day after tomorrow and you can select the photos you want. Place your order and you'll have them in a week."

"You select them," Kaden laughed. "I'm not very good at that sort of thing."

Ashley tilted her head and smiled at the way the lights from the restaurant's Christmas decorations danced in Kaden's eyes. "You've never married," she mused. "That surprises me. You're a beautiful woman, warm and charming."

"I've never met anyone I wanted to share my life with," Kaden mumbled. "I've always thought I'd get married when I had nothing better to do."

Ashley laughed. "The right person will come along one day."

I think they have, Kaden thought, *but I'm too late.*

Chapter 7

"Kaden, I need your help," Bevo settled his muscular frame into the chair on the other side of her desk. "I need to be off Friday night."

"Tell the Captain," Kaden replied. "He'll make it happen if he can."

"It's not that simple. I'm working the ninth-grade football game Friday night," Bevo retorted. "Everyone available is working it. My wife's parents are flying in, and she wants me to drive to Dallas with her to pick them up."

Kaden's ears perked up. "Ninth-grade game?"

"Yeah! Listen I'll owe you big time if you'll do this for me," Bevo added.

"Sure buddy, I'll be glad to help you out," she beamed.

##

Friday night lights, Kaden thought as she pulled her police uniform from the closet. Usually just the presence of an officer in uniform was enough to maintain control of the hyped-up football enthusiasts so the department put every available officer on campus to keep things running smoothly.

She dressed pulling her long blonde hair into a ponytail and threading it through the back of her police cap. It felt funny strapping on her police duty belt after wearing a shoulder holster for so long. Pepper spray, taser, collapsible baton, handcuffs, flashlight, radio and Glock. She groaned as she settled the twenty-pound duty belt on her hips. *I hope I don't have to chase anyone tonight*, she thought.

She checked her reflection in the mirror. There was something about being in complete uniform that made her proud.

##

Kaden met with the other officers in the football field house where they made certain all their radios were set to the same channel and they assigned sections to each officer. Kaden and her partner drew the section in front of the cheerleaders. Their main concern was the safety of the young girls.

Kaden greeted familiar faces and exchanged pleasantries with the mayor and school board members attending the game. Her gaze settled on Bryan Benton as he strolled across the football field.

Bryan stopped to flirt with the cheerleaders then headed toward the concession stand. Kaden knew Benton was a successful attorney with a big law firm that specialized in mergers and acquisitions. She wondered where Ashley was.

##

Ashley was surrounded by students excited to see their principal at the game. Parents, students and teachers were vying for the pretty brunette's attention. For the first time in a long time Ashley wished she were taller so she could see over the wall of people crowding around her. The wall of people broke, and Ashley had a clear view of Kaden Snow in all her glory.

Ashley caught her breath. *God there really is something about a woman in uniform*, she thought. Kaden was talking to the head cheerleader and the cheer coach Debbie Daniels. It was obvious the coach was flirting with the blonde officer. Ashly was shocked by the wave of jealously that flooded over her.

"Mrs. Benton," a student shook her arm. "Are you going to answer my dad?"

"Oh, I'm sorry," Ashley swallowed the lump in her throat. "I couldn't hear for all the noise. What did you say?"

Little Lester the Christmas Donkey

"I said you must be proud your campus received an exemplary rating from the state," the schoolboard member repeated. "You're the only campus in the district with the top rating."

"Oh, yes," Ashley admitted. "I'm very proud of the teachers and students."

"Nonsense," the board member quipped. "Excellence begins at the top."

"Thank you," Ashley mumbled searching the crowd for Kaden who had disappeared. "I must speak with someone. Please excuse me."

Ashly pushed through the crowd to find Kaden. *What will you say when you find her?* She thought. *It doesn't really matter I just want to see her.*

"Whoa," a familiar voice blurted as Ashley collided with the back of a firm body. "You need to be . . . Ashly, I didn't know you attended these games," Kaden lied turning to face the brunette.

Ashley found herself pressed closer to the officer by the crowd and she liked it. "I . . . I . . ." *again with the lump in my throat,* she thought.

Kaden caught her hand and pulled her on the other side of the fence with the cheer team.

"You look . . . incredible in uniform," Ashley couldn't keep her foolish mouth from saying what she was thinking.

A slow, knowing smile spread across Kaden's lips. "I'm glad you like it," she muttered. "Where are you sitting?"

Wherever I can get the best view of you, Ashley thought as her lips said, "Third row up, center field. I like to watch all the students, band, cheer team and the players."

Kaden leaned down and murmured into her ear "I'll be watching for you." The crowd went crazy as the team burst through the paper mascot and ran onto the field. Kaden lingered longer than necessary inhaling the scent of

Ashley's hair. *This is going to be one long miserable night*, she thought as her stomach did a back flip.

Chapter 8

"Where's Marylin Reese?" Kaden asked Coach Daniels. "I haven't seen her in several minutes."

"She went to the little-girls room over half an hour ago," the coach answered. "She should be back by now."

"I'll check on her," Kaden volunteered. She informed her partner of her actions and headed for the bathrooms on the other side of the concession stand.

A thorough search of the restrooms and concessions yielded no sign of Marylin. Kaden strode back to the field but stopped when movement beneath the bleachers caught her eye. She recognized Marylin Reese but couldn't get a good look at the fellow that was all over her. The two were so engrossed in their fondling of each other they didn't know Kaden was standing beside them.

"Miss Reese!" Kaden growled, "and you—" She choked, stunned to find the person groping the teen was Bryan Benton. "What the hell?"

"You get back to the squad," Kaden barked at Marilyn. "I'll deal with you later."

She whirled toward Benton. "You do realize you were crawling all over an under-aged student, don't you?"

"Hey, cool it," Benton preened. "I was just having a bit of fun."

"Yeah, well see how much fun this is!" Kaden flipped her handcuffs onto Benton's wrist before he could move then clipped the other bracelet around the steel pier of the bleachers. "I'll release you after the cheer squad has left the premises."

"You bitch," Benton raved. "You can't do this to me. Do you know who I am?"

"Yeah, you're a pervert that likes to screw little girls," Kaden stomped off.

##

It took Kaden several minutes to get her breathing under control. She was furious that Benton was fooling around with teenage girls with little concern about his wife's reputation. Jesus, the girl was on Ashley's ninth-grade campus. Knowing teen girls, Kaden was certain Marilyn was bragging about it to her friends.

When the squad took a break Kaden and Coach Daniels pulled Marilyn aside. "If I hear even a whisper about this," Kaden threatened, "I'll arrest you and your boyfriend. Am I clear?"

"Yes ma'am," Marilyn sobbed.

"What happened?" Daniels asked watching Marilyn rejoin the other cheerleaders.

"She and her boyfriend were making out under the bleachers," Kaden tried to chuckle, but it sounded more like a squawk. "I'm just trying to put the fear of God into her, so it doesn't happen again."

"I think you accomplished your goal," Debbie Daniels laughed. "What are you doing after the game? Everyone's going to Chili's. I thought you might like to join us."

"I can't," Kaden frowned. "I have to write up a report on any incidences that happened tonight, but I do appreciate the invite."

"A raincheck?" Debbie grinned.

"Sure," Kaden smiled.

##

Halftime sent a surge of people from the bleachers to the concession stands and restrooms. Ashley approached Kaden. "We're winning," she made small talk.

"You have a very good football team Principal Benton," Kaden's smile was warm and genuine. "It seems everything you touch turns into gold."

Ashley laughed. "I wish. Can I bring you something from the concession stands?"

Kaden surveyed the crowd around the stands. "I have a better idea," she said. "I have an ice chest in the field house. Cokes, Sprite and Dr. Pepper."

"I like your idea better," Ashley grinned slipping her hand through Kaden's arm.

"Have you seen Bryan?" Ashley asked as they walked across the football field. "He's supposed to meet me here. I rode over with the schoolboard president and Bryan's taking me home after the game."

Kaden covered Ashley's hand with her own, "I'm sure he'll show up. I'll keep an eye out for him when things settle down after halftime. If something has come up, I'll take you home."

"I'd like that," Ashley hugged Kaden's arm between her breasts. Kaden wondered if the brunette knew what she was doing to her.

##

They drank their sodas then returned to the field. The band was wrapping up their halftime number and the football players were waiting to run onto the field.

"We'd better walk around the end zone," Kaden suggested. "We don't want to be midfield when the Swarming Hornets run onto the field."

Kaden checked to make certain all the cheerleaders were present and accounted for then told Debbie she needed to take care of some business.

Bryan Benton was sitting on the ground playing games on his cellphone. "It's about damn time you came back," he bellowed.

"I could leave again," Kaden huffed. "Leave you here until the game's over."

"You wouldn't dare?" Benton snorted.

"Watch me," Kaden turned on her heel and walked away.

"Wait! Wait, please," Benton pleaded. "Please just release me and we'll forget this whole thing ever happened."

"I can't do that," Kaden smirked. "I'm not going to charge you as a favor to Principal Benton, but I must write it up in my report."

"Seriously?" Benton whimpered as Kaden unlocked the handcuffs. "Look, I have money. How much will it take to make you forget this ever happened?"

Kaden considered punching Benton in the throat but decided against it. "You don't have enough money to make me forget you were about to have sex with a fifteen-year-old," Kaden glowered. "Although I doubt it's the first time.

"Now go find your wife and try to act like a real man instead of a pedophile."

"There you are," Ashley tried to hide her disappointment at her husband's appearance. "I thought you'd forgotten about me."

"I got tied up," Benton croaked. "I'm running behind at the office. How much longer is this game going to take?"

"No telling," Ashley shrugged. "We both know that fifteen minutes of game time means thirty or forty minutes. And we've got two more quarters."

"I'm going to get something at the concession stand," Benton grumbled. "I haven't eaten all day."

"Bryan, you don't have to stay," Ashley tried to hide the joy she felt. "I can get someone to bring me home. That's not a problem."

"If that'll be okay," Benton jumped at the chance to leave. "I can work at the house tonight."

"Of course," Ashley agreed. "Go home. I'll catch a ride."

##

As Kaden helped Debbie herd the cheerleaders back to the school gym, Ashley caught up with them. "I do need a ride home," she whispered, "and maybe dinner."

Kaden nodded. Her entire world had just brightened. "The city's finest at your service, ma'am," she grinned. "Let me make certain every cheerleader has a parent here to pick her up."

Ashley greeted all the girls and praised them for doing a good job. Coach Daniels basked in the principal's praise. "We do work hard to encourage the players," she noted.

"You were exceptionally good tonight," Ashley complimented. "The team won."

"All of us are going to Chili's," Debbie said. "Would you like to join us?"

"Oh, no, I need to get home," Ashley smiled. "But thanks for the invitation."

Kaden and Ashley helped make certain each girl had a ride with a parent or guardian then made their way to Kaden's car.

"I'm guessing you want to go somewhere that won't bring us face to face with your students," Kaden said driving her car from the fieldhouse parking lot.

"That would be wonderful," Ashley agreed. "I've interacted with teenagers as much as I can stand for one day."

"I know a great Japanese place. It's about a twenty-minute drive," Kaden suggested. "Want to try it?"

"It sounds delightful," Ashley fastened her seatbelt.

Chapter 9

"Oh, please, no more wine," Ashley giggled as Kaden refilled her glass.

"That's the last of it," Kaden grinned signaling the waiter for their check. "We've managed to consume two bottles. As the designated driver, I agree that's enough."

"I've had the best time with you," Ashley placed her soft hand on Kaden's. "You've become a good friend, Kaden. Thank you."

Kaden bowed her head fighting to repress the fire that Ashley's touch had ignited. *I don't want to be your friend*, she thought. *I want to be your lover.*

"Ashley, I—"

"May I bring you anything else?" The waiter interrupted placing the check on the table.

"No, thank you," Kaden mumbled, glad he had saved her from embarrassing herself.

##

All the lights were on in the Benton house when Kaden pulled into the driveway. "Looks like your husband is still up," Kaden commented.

Ashley inhaled deeply. "Yes, I'm afraid he is," she mumbled. "Thank you for a wonderful evening, Kaden." She opened the car door and hurried to her front porch. She turned and waved as the front door swung open and Bryan yanked her inside.

Kaden thought about knocking on the door to make certain Ashley was okay but decided it would look suspicious. Bryan would never forgive her for handcuffing him under the bleachers. She backed from the drive and headed home determined to drive the feel of Ashley's hand on hers from her mind.

##

The next day she reverted to the typical black suit and white shirt worn by female detectives. She scrunched her long blond hair and let it hang wildly loose. *The wind will blow it all over my head anyway*, she thought as she left her home.

Doris and Clyde Freeman were waiting in the counselor's office when Kaden arrived at the school. "Is Principal Benton joining us?" Kaden asked.

"She took a personal day off," the counselor replied. She asked me to sit in your meeting with the Freeman's. I've sent someone to get Susie out of class."

"I don't understand why you're interrogating our daughter again," Doris huffed. "She told you everything she knows."

"Susie was extremely upset when I spoke with her right after Elise's abduction," Kaden explained. "I'm hoping she will recall something that will help me find Susie."

"Well, it's damn inconvenient," Clyde grumbled.

"I'm certain you'd want me to be as thorough if Susie were the one missing," Kaden pointed out.

"Yes, of course," Doris agreed. "We want to help in any way we can."

Susie reluctantly entered the room and sat in the chair next to her mother.

"Susie, I'd like for you to go over everything that happened the day Elise went missing." Kaden coaxed. "Please give me the tiniest detail even if you think it might not be important."

Susie nodded and began her story. "Elise was upset when she got on the bus that morning. Her parents were fighting as usual, and she overheard her mother tell her father to pack his bags and get out.

"She was crying and upset because she loves both her parents. We have homeroom and first period together and I could tell she was distraught.

"In third period Mr. Wayne jumped onto her because she wasn't paying attention. She started crying and ran from the room. I started to go after her, but Mr. Wayne made me sit down. He said she was just being a drama queen."

"Did you find her after class?" Kaden encouraged Susie to continue her tale.

"Yes ma'am," Susie nodded. "She said she was going to call her boyfriend and have him come get her. I didn't even know she had a boyfriend with a car, so I don't know who she was talking about."

That's probably when she called the Leland brothers, Kaden thought.

"Did you see who picked her up?" Kaden asked.

"No. I'm not sure she called anyone," Susie continued. "The lunch bell rang, and we headed for the cafeteria. Elise said she had to use the restroom and would meet me in the cafeteria. That's the last time I saw her," Susie burst into tears. "I should have stayed with her."

"Susie, do you think Elise ran away?" Kaden questioned.

"I . . . I . . . maybe," Susie sobbed.

"I appreciate you agreeing to talk with me again," Kaden stood. "You've helped me a lot."

Kaden watched the Freemans leave then turned to the counselor. "Do you know if Principal Benton is ill?"

"I don't know," the woman replied. "It is unusual for her to miss a day of school even when she is feeling bad."

Chapter 10

Kaden drove around for an hour trying to decide if she should check on Ashley. The brunette didn't answer when Kaden called her cellphone. *She must be asleep,* Kaden thought.

She decided to get a cup of coffee and head back to the precinct. Her cellphone rang and Casey Dawson's face flashed onto her screen.

"Please tell me you have Elise Mason," Kaden answered.

"No such luck," Casey piped, "but I do have some info you might be interested in."

"Do tell," Kaden jibed.

"Ashley Benton has been admitted to the Somerville County General Hospital."

"Somerville County?" Kaden questioned. "That's sixty miles from here. Why didn't she go to Holy Cross Methodist?"

"I have no idea," Casey answered. "I'm just letting you know it came up on my computer this morning."

"Thanks, Casey," Kaden said. "I owe you one."

Driving slower than usual because of the hazardous road conditions, Kaden arrived at the hospital ninety minutes later. She asked for Ashley's room number at the information desk and was told there was no such patient.

Kaden showed the woman her badge. "I'm with the police department," she added.

The volunteer wrote a room number on a piece of paper and handed it to Kaden.

"Four fifteen," Kaden mumbled as she punched the elevator number for the fourth floor. She found the room number and slowly opened the door. The room was dark with only a sliver of light slipping into the room from the bathroom.

Ashley was hooked to an IV and was sleeping. Kaden eased into the room and pulled a chair close to the bed. She planned to be there when the brunette opened her eyes. Kaden called Bevo and asked him to cover for her for a couple of hours.

"Kaden," Ashley muttered. "What are you doing here?"

"I came to see about you," Kaden replied. "What's wrong with you?"

"Nothing serious," Ashley lisped. "You shouldn't be here."

Kaden noticed the slight speech defect and turned on the night light above the bed.

"Please, no," Ashley pleaded.

Kaden gasped when she saw Ashley's face. A big bruise marked the side of her face, her lips were swollen and a cut above her eye looked wickedly painful.

"What happened?" Kaden asked but she already knew the answer. "Who did this to you?"

Ashley turned her face away and said nothing.

The door to the room opened and a young doctor entered. "Oh good, you're awake," he greeted Ashley.

"I'll wait in the hall," Kaden said slipping from the room to call Bevo. She arranged for her partner to pick up Boss and keep him until Kaden could get the dog.

"I may need to spend the night," Kaden explained.

She paced the hall as the doctor examined Ashley. After what seemed like hours the man left Ashley's room. Kaden pounced on him.

"What happened to her?" She demanded pulling back her coat to expose her badge.

"Domestic violence," the doctor replied. "I'm pretty certain her husband used her for a punching bag."

"What time was she admitted?" Kaden asked.

"Around nine this morning," the doctor checked Ashley's chart on his iPad. "She has a concussion and several contusions on her stomach and back. The one on her face is obvious."

"Who brought her in?" Kaden inquired.

The doctor consulted his iPad. "I'm not certain. You'll need to talk to admissions for that information."

"How long are you going to keep her in the hospital?' Kaden asked.

"Overnight," the doctor replied. "I want to observe her and if she does okay, I'll release her in the morning."

Kaden thanked the doctor then went downstairs to admissions. She wondered why Ashley was in this hospital instead of the one only a few miles from her home.

"It looks like she was dropped off at the emergency room door," the admissions clerk scowled. "The nurse on duty noted that a car pulled up, Mrs. Benton got out and stumbled into the emergency room. The driver pulled away. The nurse thought they had gone to park their car, but they never returned."

"She admitted herself?" Kaden mumbled.

"Yep," the clerk responded.

Kaden stopped by the cold drink machine and picked up two Dr. Peppers. One for herself and one for Ashley.

Chapter 11

"Do you want to tell me what happened?" Kaden asked settling into the chair beside Ashley's bed. "Or do I have to guess? I must warn you that what I'm guessing isn't pretty."

"What happened isn't pretty," Ashley murmured. "It hurts to talk."

"I brought Dr. Pepper," Kaden smiled pulling a straw from its wrapper. "Can you suck through this straw?"

"Yes," Ashley croaked.

Kaden raised the head of Ashley's bed and held the straw to her lips so she could drink.

"Oh my God! That's good," Ashley sighed.

"Stop me if I'm wrong," Kaden started, "but I'm guessing Bryan was mad about something last night and took it out on you."

"Aren't you the clairvoyant," Ashley groaned as her half smile hurt her lips.

"Are you going to file charges against him?" Kaden asked.

"No, I . . . I can't," Ashley sniffed.

"Why not?" Kaden queried.

"He's my husband," Ashley mumbled. "What would people say? What would Father Jamison say, what would my parents say?"

"So, you're going to continue like this until he kills you?" Kaden reasoned.

Ashley was silent turning away from the darkness in Kaden's blue eyes.

"Do you love him?" Kaden asked softly.

The long silence made Kaden think Ashley had fallen asleep. She jerked when the brunette answered.

"No," Ashley murmured. "I'm not certain I ever did. I think that's what frustrates him."

"Frustrated or not," Kaden declared, "no one has the right to beat another person."

Ashley cringed.

"He did more than beat you!" Kaden suddenly realized. "Did he rape you?"

"Kaden, please I don't want to talk about this anymore." Ashley pleaded.

Kaden rubbed her eyes trying to make some sense of the tangled thoughts running through her mind. She knew she had to get away from Ashley Benton before she said something she'd regret. "I'm going for a cup of coffee. Can I get you anything?"

"No, thank you," Ashley muttered.

Kaden left the room with her emotions in a turmoil. Half of her wanted to find Bryan Benton and beat him senseless while the other half wanted to stay at Ashley's side and protect her. She knew she'd spend the night at Ashley's bedside.

##

"Detective Snow," a gentle hand shook Kaden's shoulder. "Did you spend the night here?"

"Yes, doctor." Kaden stood stretching to get the kinks out. "I wanted to make certain no one tried to finish the job they started on Mrs. Benton."

"How is my patient this morning?" The doctor turned his attention to Ashley.

"Much better," Ashly half smiled. "I really need to get out of the hospital."

"I'm going to release you," the doctor informed her. "I must warn you Mrs. Benton, one more concussion and you could end up a vegetable. This is serious."

"I know," Ashley muttered.

"Give me about an hour and the nurse will bring a wheelchair. I assume you'll take her home, Detective Snow.

Little Lester the Christmas Donkey

"Yes," Kaden nodded.

After the doctor left Kaden searched the small closet for Ashley's clothes. She gasped when she saw they were covered with blood. "I'll be right back," she informed Ashley. "Don't leave without me."

Ashley tried to suppress her smile but couldn't. "Don't make me laugh," she said. "It hurts too much."

"I'll be right back," Kaden grinned as she left the room. *It's amazing how making her smile makes me,* happy she thought.

##

Kaden returned to the room to find Ashley sitting on the side of the bed looking perplexed.

"I found a sweatshirt and a pair of sweatpants that should fit you," Kaden pulled the items from the giftshop bag. "They'll do until we can get you home anyway."

She helped Ashley pull the shirt over her head then bent over to put the brunette's feet into the legs of the sweatpants. "Hold on to my shoulders as I straighten up," Kaden instructed. "I'll pull up the pants as you stand."

Ashley did as she was instructed and found herself pressed against Kaden as they stood. "I . . ." Ashly didn't know what possessed her. Before she could stop herself, she pressed her lips to Kaden's. It was the softest, sweetest kiss Ashley had ever known. Kaden was cognizant of Ashley's swollen lips and let the brunette lead.

"I . . . I'm sorry," Ashley muttered. "I don't know what came over me. I . . . I shouldn't have—"

Kaden wrapped her arms around the petite woman and pulled her closer, kissing her more aggressively. "Don't let me hurt your lips," she whispered as Ashley slipped her arms around Kaden's neck and kissed her hungrily.

A knock on the door tore them apart as Kaden jumped back from Ashley. The door swung open, and a wheelchair preceded the nurse into the room.

"All ready to go, Mrs. Benton" the nurse chattered. "If you'll bring your car to the admissions entrance, we'll meet you there," she instructed Kaden.

Kaden gathered Ashley's belongings and scurried from the room. *What the hell are you doing, Kaden Snow*, she chided herself as she sprinted for her car.

"Where should I take you?" Kaden asked driving the car from the hospital parking lot.

"I just called my mother," Ashley answered. "I'm going to stay with my parents for a few days."

Kaden tried to ignore the constriction in her chest. "You're welcome to stay at my place."

"I don't think that's a good idea," Ashley squirmed in her seat. "You . . . you have a strange effect on me. Maybe it's the concussion. I don't know but my mind's in chaos right now."

They chatted sporadically on the drive to Ashley's parents. Both avoiding any mention of the kiss.

"I'll help you into the house," Kaden volunteered as she parked the car.

"That's not necessary."

"Yes, it is," Kaden insisted. "I'm a public servant and it's my duty to make certain you are delivered into your parent's house safely."

Kaden stepped from her car and walked to the passenger side to help Ashley out. She got Ashley's things from the back seat then offered Ashley her arm for support. By the time they reached the door Ashley's mother was opening it.

"Come in Detective Snow," Joy Chase held open the door for them to enter.

"Mrs. Joy," Kaden exclaimed to the Library Director. "You never mentioned that Principal Benton was your daughter."

Little Lester the Christmas Donkey

"I only had occasion to visit with you when you were researching something," Joy Chase smiled, "so I didn't bother you with family matters.

"Why didn't Bryan pick you up from the hospital?" Joy turned her attention to her daughter.

"He had some big negotiation going on today," Ashley lied. "Detective Snow was kind enough to drive me home."

"I'm making lunch," Joy enthused, "Please join us, Kaden?"

"I truly must get back to the station," Kaden excused herself. "I'm just glad I was at the hospital when Principal Benton was released."

"Please, call me Ashley. Principal Benton sounds so stuffy."

Kaden nodded. They'd done enough smoke screening for Ashley's mother.

Joy Chase walked Kaden to the door returning to fuss over her daughter. "I suppose you walked into another door," Joy commented.

"Something like that," Ashley mumbled

"Mom, I didn't know you were friends with Kaden." Ashley wanted to talk about the woman who had invaded her mind and taken up residence there.

"I've known Kaden since she was in high school," Joy answered. "I watched her struggle through college working fulltime in patrol and carrying the maximum number of hours allowed so she could graduate quickly. She's a fine young woman. She'll be a good friend for you."

Chapter 12

"Where've you been?" Bevo rushed to Kaden as she placed her Glock into her desk drawer. "I thought you'd be in on time this morning."

"It's personal," Kaden growled. "But thanks for covering for me, Bro."

"Captain is looking for you," Bevo whispered. "I told him you were following up a lead on the Mason girl."

Kaden strolled to the Captain's office. "You needed me, sir?" She asked.

"Kaden fill me in on the disappearance of the Mason girl," Captain Jeff Token instructed.

"My instincts tell me she's a run-away," Kaden shrugged.

"I need more than your instincts," Token barked. "I have a meeting with the chief this afternoon and he is specifically asking about this case."

"He's taking a personal interest?" Kaden raised a questioning brow.

"Yeah," Token grimaced. "The girl's parents are holding a press conference in the morning. We're trying to get ahead of this."

"Oh, jeez," Kaden huffed. "Captain I'm fairly certain the girl ran away because her parents fight all the time. Her best friend said Elise was upset because she was afraid her parents were going to divorce."

"Evidence," Token breathed. "I need hard evidence, Kaden."

"I've got to follow up on something, Captain," Kaden said. "I'll let you know if it pans out."

Token nodded as his best detective turned to leave his office. "Kaden, I need something fast. Don't let me down."

##

Kaden left the precinct, went by Bevo's house to pick up Boss then headed back to the Somerville County Hospital. "One more concussion," the doctor had said. That meant Ashley had previous concussions. She couldn't get Ashley Benton out of her mind, and it was screwing with her head. She replayed the kiss over and over. *Ashley instigated it*, she thought. *She must care for me.*

Kaden left her car at valet parking and hurried to the records department trying to recall the name Casey Dawson had given her.

"How may I help you," a pretty redhead wearing a name tag that said, Loretta looked up from a stack of x-rays.

Loretta, Kaden thought. *Yes, Loretta is the name.*

Kaden showed Loretta her badge. "Casey Dawson told me to ask for you," Kaden informed her. "I need help with past information on a patient."

"Name?" Loretta cut to the chase.

"Uh, Kaden Snow," Kaden said.

"That's the name of the patient?" An impish smile crossed her lips.

"Oh, uh no," Kaden stammered then grinned. "That's my name. The patient is Ashley Benton."

Loretta typed several lines into her computer then frowned. "Oh," she gasped.

"What?" Kaden demanded.

"You should step around here and peruse this file yourself."

Kaden sat down in the chair Loretta vacated and began scrolling through the case records on Ashley Benton. Ashley had been admitted to the hospital nine times during the last five years. There had been broken ribs, numerous contusions and cuts, black eyes and stab wounds on one occasion. The photos turned Kaden's stomach. *How could a man beat a woman like that?* She thought. *And why in hell's name hadn't someone done something about it?*

The frequency of the beatings had increased each year going from one their first year of marriage to four in the past year. *These are just the ones that were bad enough to hospitalize her*, Kaden thought inhaling deeply.

Kaden thanked Loretta and gave the woman her card. "If I can ever be of help to you just call that number. It's my cellphone."

Kaden drove to a roadside park and took Boss for a walk. She talked to the dog as if he were human. "Boss, I've gotten myself into a mess," she said out loud. "I've fallen in love with a married woman who will never leave her husband. I wonder if she has any idea how perverted he is."

Chapter 13

Kaden tried to push Ashley from her mind as she made a bacon and scrambled-egg sandwich. She cooked two eggs for Boss who leaned against her leg affectionately. "I've missed you too big guy," she squatted and hugged his huge head between her breasts. "I'm sorry about leaving you with Bevo last night."

She carried her sandwich and a Dr. Pepper to the sofa and clicked on the TV. She patted the chair beside her where Bevo always slept but he waited for an invitation before jumping on the furniture. The big dog quickly responded and curled up beside Kaden.

The evening news was filled with the Mason's press conference. The couple blamed everyone from the City Sanitation Director to the Police Chief for their daughter's disappearance.

"She used that Chromebook thingy—the school system hands out to all the kids—to meet someone online," Calvin Mason accused.

Why do parents never accept responsibility for their own poor parenting, Kaden thought as she listened to the Mason's whine.

Kaden channel surfed for a few more minutes then tossed the remote control onto the end table beside her recliner. She tried to calm the turmoil that was raging in her mind and body. Ashley obviously liked her. Ashley was married. Ashley had kissed her soundly. Ashley wasn't a lesbian. She needed to stay away from Ashley Benton. She couldn't wait to see Ashley Benton.

Kaden's mind vacillated back and forth like a fast tennis game. The ringing of her phone pulled her out of her head.

"Kaden," she barked into the phone.

"Kaden, this is Ashley," a soft voice hummed into her ear, and she caught her breath.

"Are you okay?" Kaden asked. "Is anything wrong?"

"I just wanted to hear your voice," Ashley said.

Kaden fought to remain cool, calm and collected. "It's nice to hear your voice too," she smiled into the phone. "How are you feeling?

"Like I need some fresh air," Ashley chortled.

"Would you like to go for a ride?" Kaden asked praying the brunette would say yes.

"I'd like that very much," Ashley responded. "Fifteen minutes?"

"I'll be there," Kaden suppressed a whoop of joy. "I'll be there."

##

Exactly fifteen minutes later Ashley stepped onto the front porch of the Chase home. The door opened and Ashley walked out. "My parents are sleeping in front of the TV," she giggled as she locked the front door. "I left them a note in case they awaken while I'm gone."

Kaden studied Ashley's face by the front porch light. "You look much better than when I left you."

"I am," Ashley nodded. "I've slept all day. Let's get into your car."

Kaden held Ashley's elbow until they reached the car. "Honestly Kaden I'm fine."

"Kaden fastened her seatbelt. Do you want to go somewhere for a drink or—"

"Let's pull through a drive thru for a cold drink," Ashley suggested. Then just drive around looking at Christmas lights. "There is a gorgeous cul-de-sac in Castle Hills that will take your breath away."

"I'd love that," Kaden grinned pulling into a Sonic Drive Thru.

Little Lester the Christmas Donkey

They drove through brightly lighted neighborhoods exclaiming over the beautiful displays of lights and nativity scenes. They laughed and sang Christmas Carols ranging from "Rudolph the Red Nosed Reindeer" to "O Holy Night."

"I want to show you something," Kaden beamed as she drove to the highest hill on the outskirts of their hometown. She pulled her car to the edge and turned off the engine.

"It's beautiful," Ashley gasped. "Just beautiful."

Kaden slipped her hand into her pocket and pulled out a key on a small chain. "This is the key to my home. If you ever need to go somewhere safe where Bryan wouldn't dare follow you use this. You can let yourself in even if I'm not home."

"Thank you," Ashley whispered.

They sat in silence surveying the lighted wonderland below them. "I never knew such a view existed," Ashley enthused. "Do you bring all your girlfriends here?"

"You're the only person I've ever brought here," Kaden murmured leaning over to turn Ashley's face toward hers. "I've never cared enough about anyone to share this with them.

Ashley leaned into Kaden's lips. "I've never kissed a woman before," she whispered against warm soft lips. "I like it." Ashley slid her hand behind Kaden's neck pulling her closer, kissing her as if her life depended on it.

Ashley moaned, her breath coming in short fast wisps as she pulled Kaden on top of her, clutching Kaden to her. Ashley's lips were full and firm. She moved them slowly against Kaden's lips stealing her soul. She slipped her tongue between Kaden's teeth and sought the blonde's tongue. "Oh, dear God, you taste as good as I knew you would," Ashley whimpered.

Kaden pulled away and sat back in her seat.

"What's wrong?" Ashley murmured. "Don't you want me?"

"More than anything in the world," Kaden assured her. "But what then, Ashley. What about tomorrow. Will you leave Bryan and eventually make a life with me? What, exactly are you offering me? I don't want to be your spur of the moment fling. I want to be your happily ever after."

"Of course," Ashley sighed. "I'm being unfair to you. I got carried away. I'm so sorry."

"So, no future for us?" Kaden rasped "Not even an effort?"

"Kaden, I want you so badly I can taste it," Ashley moaned, "but I can't turn my life upside down. My job, my place in the community for a . . ." Ashley's voice trailed off.

"Lesbian relationship," Kaden finished Ashley's sentence.

Ashley nodded her head. "I've been promised the superintendent's job when Mr. Fellows retires next year. I've worked all my life for that. There's no way I'd get that job if people knew I was a lesbian."

"No one cares about your sex life anymore," Kaden argued. "Look at all the homosexuals that are being elected to public office."

"It's different in education," Ashley hung her head. "I know they give a lot of lip service to sexual preference not mattering anymore, but that's not true. I've been in closed-door meetings where qualified teachers were passed over for good promotions and talked about behind their back because they were homosexuals. I'm sorry, Kaden."

"Did you know I was a lesbian?" Kaden asked.

"No, it never crossed my mind," Ashley answered truthfully. "You look very feminine. You know makeup, earrings. You look like a beautiful model."

"I've never announced to the world that I like women," Kaden continued. "No one thinks I'm a lesbian but you and that's only because I returned your kiss.

"What's your point?" Ashley frowned.

"My point is that leaving Bryan doesn't mean anyone will think less of you. I don't mind staying in the closet. Hell, I've been there all my life."

"I . . . I can't," Ashley wiped a tear from her cheek. "I just can't."

Kaden started her car and drove Ashley home. She walked her to the door and turned to leave as Ashley unlocked the door.

"Kaden," Ashley caught her hand, "this has been one of the—no, the happiest night of my life. Thank you." She opened the door and disappeared inside the house.

Kaden strode to her car. *From now on it's just going to be Boss and me*, she promised herself.

Chapter 14

Kaden strapped on the harness so she could keep up with Boss. If he locked onto a scent the harness was the only thing that made it possible for her to hold onto him. They were going hunting today. Captain Token had issued her an ultimatum—either solve the Mason case or turn it over to someone else. The Masons had hired an attorney and were on the verge of filing a lawsuit against the city and the school district. Kaden had never had a case taken away from her. She wasn't about to start now.

Kaden formulated a plan as she drove to the school. Today was the last day of school until after New Year's. If she didn't find Elise today the teen would be locked in the school for the next two weeks with no access to the kitchen and no way out of the school.

Kaden entered the school office and greeted the secretary. "I'm cleared to be here all day with my dog," she said.

"Yep, I've got the memo right here," the secretary fanned the air with a sheet of paper. "You just do your thing and yell if I can do anything for you."

"Is the Cafeteria Manager here?" Kaden asked.

"Other side of the cafeteria," the woman gestured across the wide expanse of tables and chairs in the glass-enclosed cafeteria, "middle door."

"Martha, I need a copy of . . ." Ashley stopped mid-sentence when she saw Kaden. "Good morning Detective Snow," she smiled. "I understand you're going to be with us all day."

"Or until I finish," Kaden quipped. "Whichever comes first."

Ashley nodded. "Let Martha know if you need anything."

Kaden nodded and headed Boss in the direction of the kitchen.

Cafeteria Manager Roberta Reed was in her office going over menus when Kaden entered. "Whoa, you can't bring that dog in here!" Roberta blurted.

"He's cleared to go anywhere," Kaden insisted. "He's probably more sterile than anyone in this building."

"Sorry," Roberta laughed uneasily. "That was just a knee-jerk reaction to an animal in my kitchen. You know rules and inspectors and all that."

"Yeah, I know," Kaden agreed. "You filed a theft report yesterday. Could you tell me what was stolen and how long food has been disappearing?"

"I first noticed it about two weeks ago," Roberta said pulling a yellow legal pad from her desk drawer. Bread, lunch meat, fruit, chips that sort of thing. Just enough for a meal." She pushed the pad toward Kaden. "It's all there with the dates."

"Boss and I are going to work," Kaden informed her. "We'll stay out of your way.

Kaden gave Boss the scent of Elise Mason and the dog instantly went to work. He sniffed all over the school. The scent seemed to be everywhere. Kaden was certain Elise Mason was hiding in the school and stealing food from the lunchroom to survive.

##

When the last bell rang and the last student cleared the halls, the custodians began locking doors. An exhausted Kaden slid down the wall and sat on the floor. Boss lay down beside her, his head in her lap. She leaned her head back against the wall and tried to think of any place they hadn't searched in the school.

Ashley stood silently watching Kaden resting against the wall. It took all the strength she had to refrain from crawling into the blonde's lap. She hadn't seen Kaden in two weeks, two long, miserable weeks. Kaden had taken up residence in her head. She was the first thing Ashley thought of each morning and her last thought before she fell asleep each night. She quietly backed into the office and closed the door. Loving Kaden Snow would cost her too much.

##

A scream jerked Kaden from her sleep. She jumped to her feet and looked around trying to ascertain where she was. *The school*, she thought. *I fell asleep.*

Boss was pawing at the door between the hallway and the foyer leading into the principal's office. A second scream and Boss threw his massive body against the door.

Kaden ran to the door and opened it. The sound of breaking glass and splintering furniture came from Ashley's office. Kaden grabbed Boss' harness and held on for dear life as he dragged her into the fray.

They burst into the office just as Bryan Benton was bringing a heavy trophy down on his wife. "Don't ever ask me for a divorce again, bitch," Bryan shrieked.

Kaden released Boss and the Rottweiler lunged catching Bryan's arm on the downswing. Boss clamped down hard on Bryan's arm as the dog's weight drove the man to the floor yanking his arm from its socket.

Kaden sprang into action. Taking photos with her cellphone to document the fight. Ashley moaned as Kaden called an ambulance and Bevo.

Bryan was screaming as if he were dying and he probably wished he was. "Hold" Kaden commanded Boss and the dog buried his teeth deeper into Bryan's arm bringing additional shrieks of pain from the man's lips.

Kaden knelt beside the unconscious Ashley to examine her injuries. The words of the Somerville County Hospital doctor rang in her head. "One more concussion and you could become a vegetable."

Little Lester the Christmas Donkey

"Please let her be okay," Kaden prayed out loud.

"Bitch," Bryan stopped shrieking long enough to cuss at her. "Get this monster off me."

Kaden stood. "Not a snowball's chance in hell," she smirked. "Hold Boss."

Boss clamped down harder bringing louder screams of agony from Bryan.

Bevo burst through the door ahead of the medics. "Are you okay?" He yelled over Bryan's shrieks.

"I'm fine," Kaden answered. "If you'll take care of him, I'll follow the ambulance to the hospital and try to get a statement from Principal Benton. He probably needs medical treatment too. Boss was a little rough with him. He was trying to kill his wife and Boss saved her."

"Release Boss," Kaden commanded. Boss let go of Benton then darted down the hallway disappearing around a corner.

"What the hell?" Kaden yelled. "Boss."

"There was a girl at the end of the hallway," the medic volunteered. "Your dog took off after her."

"Elise Mason," Kaden yelled. "You got this Bevo?"

"I've got it," Bevo responded. "Go get that damn girl."

Chapter 15

Kaden skidded around the corner as Boss began scratching at the door of the supply closet. "Sit," she commanded. Boss backed from the door and sat on the floor never taking his eyes off Kaden.

Kaden slowly opened the door. It was dark and smelled of cleaning supplies. "Elise are you in here?" she called.

Only silence greeted her as she moved into the dark room. Shelves lined the walls, and one double sided shelf ran down the center. A small sniffle caught her attention. "Boss," she motioned for him to enter, "do you hear what I hear?"

Boss eased in front of Kaden and moved toward the corner. Elise was huddled on the floor trying to make herself as small as possible.

Kaden stood in front of her. "Elise, look at me."

Elise began to cry as her gaze moved from the detective's feet to her kind face. "Give me your hand sweetheart." Kaden held out her hand to the teen. "Everything's going to be okay."

Elise's small hand reached out for Kaden's, and she allowed the blonde to pull her to her feet. Elise burst into tears. "I've been so scared," she wailed. "My parents will kill me."

Kaden slipped her arm around Elise's trembling shoulders. "No one's going to kill you. Let's get you out of here."

"You don't understand," Elise insisted. "This entire thing was my father's idea."

The medics were putting Ashley into the ambulance when Kaden led Elise to the group. "Bevo, meet Elise Mason our missing girl," Kaden introduced them. Her heart wanted to follow Ashley to the hospital, but her mind knew she should stay with the scared teenager. "Boss and I are taking her to the station. I'll notify Captain Token on the way."

"I can handle this," Bevo nodded. "There's another ambulance on the way for Bryan Benton. Boss almost tore his arm off."

"Yeah, sorry about that," Kaden smirked.

##

"Bevo and I have Elise Mason," Kaden reported to Captain Token. "I thought you might want to notify her parents and the news media. I'm bringing Elise to the station. Bevo is taking Ashley and Bryan Benton to the hospital. He needs to get their statements and arrest Bryan for attempted murder."

"You can fill me in when you get here," Token ordered.

"Elise, honey," Kaden spoke softly, "why have you hidden out in the school for the past three weeks?"

Elise bowed her head, wiped the tears from her cheek and began to talk. "I met a boy online. At least I thought it was a boy. He turned out to be a gross old man. My father caught me and came up with the idea of making it look like I'd been kidnapped. My Mom knows nothing about any of this.

"I knew it was wrong, but my Dad said we needed the money and things would get better at home if we had money. He said he wouldn't leave Mom and me.

"He said the school district and city would settle to avoid going to court. It'd be no big deal and we'd be rich.

"He took over communicating with the guy in the chatroom and lured him to the school so the security cameras would record it.

"The longer I hid the harder it became to show my face. I stole food from the lunchroom and watched TV at night in the audio/video classroom, so I knew there was a big search going on for me. Then I saw my parents were going to sue the city and I knew I had to come forward. I just didn't know how."

"I thought the school was closed for Christmas holidays and was on my way to the cafeteria to get something to eat when I heard glass breaking. I looked around the corner and your dog saw me."

"This should be fun," Kaden shook her head wondering how Token would react.

##

Kaden sneaked Elise into the station through the tunnel from the parking garage. News vans had already begun to gather in front of the station.

"Captain," Kaden led Elise into Token's office. "I brought Elise here in case you want to speak with her before you face the news hawks. May I speak with you alone?"

Token walked from his office closing the door behind him so Elise wouldn't overhear their conversation. "What's up?" He asked cautiously.

Kaden relayed the information Elise had given her. "You need to talk to her family before you turn Elise over to them," Kaden advised. "The kid's scared to death of her father."

A loud roar from the crowd that had gathered outside the precinct made them walk to the front of the building. The Masons were already holding their own press conference.

"We are delighted to see all of you," Calvin Mason yelled into a microphone held in front of him by a reporter. "I want to officially announce that we have filed a lawsuit against the city, the police department, and the school district. We hold them 100% responsible for our daughter's disappearance."

Little Lester the Christmas Donkey

"Didn't you tell them we have Elise?" Kaden turned to Token.

"I might have failed to mention it," Token grinned. "Watch and learn Kaden. Oh, go get Elise."

Token strode to the newswoman and took her mic. "How much will you be suing us for," he asked Calvin.

"Millions," the man screamed.

"Be sure to get enough to cover the cost of wasted man hours, overtime, vehicle use and . . ."

"What the hell are you talking about?" Calvin shrieked.

"The bill you will receive from us for a fraudulent missing person's report." Token smirked. "Of course, we'll provide you with room and board for the next ten years."

Kaden escorted Elise to the Captain.

"My baby," Marlene Mason shrieked joyously wrapping her arms around Elise. "Our baby, Calvin. They've found her. This is all I want for Christmas."

Calvin Mason turned an unusual shade of green.

"What's going on?" The newswoman demanded.

"We're not certain," Token said. "We're still trying to sort things out. For right now I can tell you the case has taken an unusual turn."

##

Kaden and Token led the Mason family and their lawyer into an interrogation room. "Why don't you tell us everything starting from the beginning? Captain Token instructed Calvin.

"My daughter was kidnapped, and your people did nothing to—"

"I don't want to hear the story you fabricated," Token growled. "I want to hear the truth."

"That is the truth," Calvin snapped.

Token repeated the story Elise had told them. "What do you have to say for yourself?" Token scowled at Calvin.

"That's preposterous," Calvin screamed. "You didn't tell them a lie like that, did you honey? Did you?"

Elise shook her head no and Kaden could see a reversal of her statement coming.

"Mr. Mason, things will go a lot easier on you," Token said, "if you just tell us the truth."

"I have told you the truth—"

"Excuse me Captain," Kaden interrupted. "We don't need his statement. I recorded Elise's statement in the car. She was under no duress just terrified of her father's wrath. I'm certain the public and the prosecutor will believe her. It's obvious Mr. Mason is lying."

"I'm out of here," Mason's attorney stood. "I'm not a criminal lawyer. I can't represent you. You'll get my final bill in the next few days."

"I want a plea bargain," Calvin harped. "I want—"

"The longer you yammer, the more time you will serve," Token got in the man's face. "You have one final chance to tell me the truth. After that I'm throwing the book at you."

"Okay," Calvin caved.

Token turned on the audio/video to record the man's confession.

Kaden followed Token back to his office as officers led Calvin to booking and Marlene and Elise to the waiting room

"Shoot that audio to my phone," Token instructed Kaden. We may not need it, but it never hurts to have back up."

"I hope we won't need it," Kaden grinned, "because I don't have it. I was so concerned about Elise I didn't record her statement."

Token laughed. "You've done a good day's work Kaden. Take Boss and go home."

Chapter 16

Kaden entered the hospital through the emergency room doors. "Can you tell me where Ashley Benton is?" She asked the admitting clerk.

The woman checked her computer. "Mrs. Benton was treated and released," she informed Kaden.

"She wasn't badly hurt?" Kaden breathed a sigh of relief.

"A couple of cuts and bruises but no broken bones or concussion." The woman replied.

Kaden thanked the clerk and walked to her car. *Ashley probably went to her parents,* she thought. She debated visiting the brunette then decided it would be okay.

Boss was sleeping in the seat beside her and she caressed the head of the dog she loved so much. "You saved a life today, big guy," she muttered.

Kaden smiled when Joy Chase opened the door. "Kaden it's good to see you again," Joy bubbled. "Is everything okay?"

"I'm looking for Ashley," Kaden said. "I thought she might be here."

"No, I haven't seen her today," Joy said. "Have you tried calling her?"

"That's the problem," Kaden fabricated. "She left her phone at school and I'm trying to get it to her. I'll just run by her home and leave it there if she isn't home. Sorry I bothered you."

"No bother and Kaden, have a Merry Christmas."

"Merry Christmas to you, Joy," Kaden forced a smile.

"Damn," Kaden cursed as she backed from the Chase driveway. "Damn, she's gone home to Bryan." Kaden wondered what she had done that was so bad God had chosen to punish her with unrequited love.

As Kaden pulled her car into the garage Boss emitted a low guttural growl. "What's wrong, Boss?"

She felt the small hairs on the back of her neck stand up. She drew her gun as she stepped from the vehicle. Boss jumped over the console and exited her side putting himself between Kaden and danger.

They moved forward together. Kaden keyed in the access code to open the door between her home and the garage. The door slowly swung open. A mouth-watering aroma filled Kaden's senses. Woman and dog advanced toward the delectable smell. Christmas music filled the house with happy sounds.

Boss was the first to see her. He lunged toward Ashley and hummed when she stroked between his ears. "Where's your girl, big fellow?" Ashley murmured looking up to lock gazes with Kaden.

Kaden stood still afraid she'd make the scene before her disappear. She had dreamed of Ashley in her kitchen, but knew it was too good to be true. *Maybe I took a blow to the head today*, she thought.

"Are you just going to stand there?" Ashley smiled.

"I . . . I," Kaden stammered. "What are you doing here?"

"I thought you might like a home-cooked meal and I brought you a Christmas present," Ashley beamed walking to the kitchen island and picking up a brightly wrapped package.

"Are you okay?" Kaden asked moving toward her. "The hospital, they said—"

"I'm just fine," Ashley tiptoed to brush her lips against Kaden's. "Open the present."

Kaden pulled the ribbon from the gift and removed the wrapping paper around the flat box. "Is it an oversized book?" Kaden guessed.

"No," Ashley smiled.

Kaden lifted the lid from the box. It contained two matching gold frames. Kaden caught her breath when she realized that she held framed photographs from the night they had dined at Outback. "They're beautiful," she murmured. "Just beautiful."

"I think they will look incredible right here," Ashley walked to the buffet in Kaden's dining room and placed the photos among the Christmas holly.

Kaden looked at the setting. "It's lovely."

Ashley slid her arms around Kaden's waist and tilted her head back. "A thank-you kiss would be nice," she teased.

Slowly Kaden wrapped her arms around the brunette lowering her lips to Ashley's. She didn't close her eyes afraid the dream would disappear. She moaned as Ashley's tongue moved along her lower lip then asked permission to enter her mouth. After a long breath-taking kiss Kaden pulled back.

"I didn't get you a Christmas present," she admitted. "I have nothing for you."

"There's nothing you want to give me?" Ashley smirked salaciously. "Nothing you'd like to do to me?"

"Well . . . maybe there is something I'd like to give you," Kaden whispered in her ear. "But what I truly want to see is both of us together in one photo as a couple."

Mariah Carey's "All I want For Christmas Is You," filled the room with upbeat music.

"Do you hear what I hear?" Kaden murmured against Ashley's lips.

"Yes, darling. They're playing our song," Ashley hummed. "All I want for Christmas is you, Kaden Snow."

Merry Christmas – The End

Little Lester the Christmas Donkey

Little Lester the Christmas Donkey

Learn more about Erin Wade

Website: https://www.erinwade.us

#1 Best Selling Books & Audios by Erin Wade

Too Strong to Die
Death Was Too Easy
Three Times as Deadly
Branded Wives
Living Two Lives
Don't Dare the Devil
The Roughneck & the Lady
Wrongly Accused
The Destiny Factor
Shakespeare Under Cover
Assassination Authorized
Two Ways to Die, Book #1 – A Java Jarvis Thriller
Mardi Gras Ghost, Book #2 – A Java Jarvis Thriller
Another Cup of Java, Book #3 – A Java Jarvis Thriller
Do You Hear What I Hear? – Short Story
Cupid's Crossbow – Short Story
A Woman to Die For
The Littlest Werewolf - Short Story
The Trinket – Short Story
Barbed Wire
Haunting Vanity – Short Story
The Table Between Us – Short Story
Dark Justice, Book #1 - God's Canyon
Dark Justice, Book #2 - Garden of Eden
Dark Justice, Book #3 – Buried Secrets
Riding the Storm
The Hotel
You Ring My Bell – Short Story
A Kick in the Heart – Short Story
A Valentine for Robbie – Short Story
Please Lie to me
The Dark Side of Midnight
Here's to You, Mrs. Anderson
Who Wrote the Thriller Anyway?
Little Lester the Christmas Donkey
Coming in 2025
Promise Me Tomorrow
Doomsday Cruise
Firestorm

Little Lester the Christmas Donkey

Made in the USA
Columbia, SC
28 December 2024